BROKEN RECORD

2/15

BROKEN RECORD

K.A. LINDE

Visit my website at
www.kalinde.com

Join my newsletter for free books and exclusive content!
www.kalinde.com/subscribe

Cover Designer: Okay Creations.
www.okaycreations.com
Photographer: Perrywinkle Photography,
www.perrywinklephoto.com
Editor: Unforeseen Editing,
www.unforeseenediting.com

ISBN-13: 978-1948427333

Bad Habits

Lucas Atwood stepped over the threshold of Savannah's parents' two-story home. He looked even taller than when she had last seen him. He easily towered over everyone in the room and drew her eyes like a moth to a flame. He'd cut his hair. The shaggy locks she'd adored for years were gone. The crisp button-down and khaki pants were a sharp departure from his typical basketball attire.

He looked…good.

And she should never have noticed.

"Savannah?" her boyfriend, Easton, said at her side.

"Yeah?" She drew her attention away from Lucas. "Did I miss something?"

Easton flashed her a smile. Sometimes, it was hard to believe that they'd been dating for nearly three years. That she was finally graduating from the

University of North Carolina-Chapel Hill and going off into the real world to be a reporter. At *The Washington Post*, no less.

"I asked if you wanted another drink."

She glanced down at the empty glass she'd been holding. When had she finished it?

"Uh, yeah. Sure. That would be great."

He kissed her cheek. "Be right back."

She watched him go with a half-smile painted on her cherry-red lips. This was her official college graduation party. The one her parents had thrown for family and close friends. It was the party where she had to play the part of perfect Savannah Maxwell, senator's daughter. A role that she had worn like a second skin her entire life. Sometimes, she wasn't even able to recognize the difference between that part and the real Savannah Maxwell.

Everyone said that she'd gone through a rebellious stage once she finally got out of high school. Even though UNC was only ten minutes down the road from her family home, she wasn't living under their roof anymore, and she didn't have any of their rules.

Then, she had started dating Easton, and everyone was so happy to see that phase end. Easton was everything she had ever wanted in a boyfriend— college tennis player, smart, funny, kind, caring, loyal. If only he didn't want to be a politician. Just like her father and brother. She knew it was unfair to be frustrated by his choice in careers, but she'd had enough of politics for one lifetime. But if she wanted Easton, then she had to take that part of him too.

"Deep in thought?"

Savannah snapped her head to the side and found Lucas with a half-smile, staring back at her. "Hey."

"Penny for your thoughts?"

She tried to hide the smile from her face but was unsuccessful. That had been a catch phrase between them since eighth grade. She'd been upset over some stupid boy after school. Lucas picked up a stray penny in the parking lot and placed it in her palm. She divulged everything that had happened, and the phrase had stuck around.

"No," she told him.

He pulled his hands out of his pockets to show they were empty. "That's good, I suppose. Fresh out of pennies."

Her cheeks heated as he took a step closer to her. His eyes were bright blue, and without his hair falling into his face, she could see how electric they were in the light of the foyer. But being around Lucas was a bad idea.

She took a step away from him. "What are you doing here, Lucas?"

"Your parents invited me," he said casually.

"Isn't your graduation next weekend? Shouldn't you be studying for finals?"

He shrugged. "We made it to the NCAA tournament. I think I'm going to pass my finals."

"I'm sure. Padding your grades much?"

Lucas played basketball for Vanderbilt, and he was good. Really good. Better than Savannah's brother Brady and his own brother, Chris, who had both played at UNC when they went there. Then, Lucas had turned traitor and gone to Vandy. It still made her cringe.

"We both know that they don't need to."

She laughed softly. Of course they didn't need to. For all his dumb jock tendencies, he'd graduated second in their high school class—she was first. He'd gotten to give the speech to introduce her. Most of the audience had been crying from laughter before she even got onto the stage.

If only everything was still like that between them. If only it hadn't unequivocally changed the summer after graduation.

"So, did your parents fly you in just for the party?" she asked.

He hadn't been at the ceremony in Kenan Memorial Stadium where she dressed in Carolina blue and walked with all of her friends. None of who were here at this stuffy get-together.

"Yeah. I wanted to be here for you. But my flight got delayed, and so…I'm late."

"Oh."

Lucas glanced over her shoulder, frowned, and took a step back. She followed his gaze and found

Easton meandering toward her. His eyes narrowed when he saw her talking to Lucas.

"Hey, here's your drink," Easton said, passing her a sweet tea vodka and lemonade.

"Thanks." She took it from him and absentmindedly sipped it as she bathed in awkwardness to the nth degree.

Easton, ever the gentleman, stuck his hand out. "Hey, Lucas. I didn't know you were going to be here."

They shook.

"Last-minute trip," Lucas told him.

"Just for graduation?"

"Yeah. I have to finish up finals next week."

"What's your degree in again?" Easton asked.

"Business."

"Right," Easton said. "What are you doing with that after graduation?"

Lucas shrugged. "Depends on the draft, I suppose."

"Draft?" Savannah asked, finally interjecting into the conversation.

"Uh…yeah. Figure I'll just keep playing ball until they tell me I can't."

"You could go anywhere," Savannah said. Her heart in her throat.

"Well, yeah. That's kind of how a draft works."

Easton grinned like a Cheshire cat and put his

arm around Savannah. "That will be good for you. New city. New team. That sort of thing."

Lucas just laughed. "Yeah. We'll see what happens. I'm going to go check out the rest of the party."

He nodded at them both and then disappeared through the living room. Savannah felt a weight lift off of her chest. Easton just shook his head.

"I really don't like that guy," Easton said. His eyes were still on Lucas's back as he drifted around the room.

"Let's not today, okay?"

Easton had every reason not to like Lucas. To hate him even. But she really did not want to get into it. She'd chosen Easton. She had pushed Lucas out of her life. That should be enough for him.

"Yeah. Sorry," Easton said, rubbing a hand up and down her back. "I just can't believe he even showed up."

"I've known him since I was a baby. Our parents are best friends. It's not that surprising."

She took another long drink and then veered into the living room. Easton followed and thankfully didn't press the issue.

Savannah tried to push away the awkwardness as she mingled with her parents' friends and went through all the pleasantries. She was really looking forward to the after-party on Franklin Street. The rest of the newspaper had gotten together a going-away event for all the seniors. Guaranteed to be better than this party.

"Hey you!"

Savannah whirled around and found her sister-in-law Liz Dougherty standing in front of her. "Oh my God!" Savannah cried, throwing her arms around Liz.

They'd worked on the paper together when Liz was a senior at UNC, during the debacle with her older brother Brady while he was running for Congress. Liz was probably her closest girlfriend. It *sucked*, having her in DC. One more reason to be stoked that she was moving.

"How are you? And congratulations!" Liz said. "I'm so proud of you! *Washington Post*!"

"Thank you. Thank you. I'm good. So ready to move already."

"I know that feeling. And finally moving in with Easton, huh?" Liz waggled her brows up and down.

Savannah laughed. "Yeah. Lucky that Brady had an opening in his staff."

"Lucky." Liz snorted. "He's your boyfriend. Of course there's going to be room."

"*Nepotism* was the first word that came to mind," Savannah said with a laugh.

"Eh. Whatever. If it makes you happy, then we'll let the boys deal with the potential consequences." Liz giggled and drew her away from the center of the room. Then, she stopped laughing and frowned. "So, are you going to tell me what's really going on? Because you look like you swallowed a toad."

Savannah checked her reaction. Why the hell was she upset? This should be one of the happiest days of her life. Yet Liz had seen what she'd been trying to ignore. She wasn't okay. She felt like she was barely floating above the water.

"I don't know."

"Is it Lucas?" Liz asked, glancing over Savannah's shoulder.

"No," Savannah said quickly. Maybe…too quickly.

Liz raised an eyebrow. "Have y'all talked since last summer?"

Savannah shook her head. "I don't want to talk."

"You can't avoid him forever."

"Why not? That makes everything so much easier."

"Lucas is a part of your life whether you want him there or not. You can't run away from your problems, Savi."

She took long sip of her drink. "I can try."

Liz shot her a *don't kid yourself* look. "Take it from somebody who knows. I tried to erase my problems for over a year. It was not pretty. And I don't want that for you."

Savannah sighed. "I know."

"At the very least, it's best to get it all out of the

way before you come to live by me. That way, you have a clean slate."

"I'm so ready to live near you again," Savannah said.

"Me too. It's going to be the best." Liz hip-checked her and then sauntered off toward Savannah's oldest brother, Brady.

He was chatting with their parents, but when his eyes fell on Liz, the world stopped. Savannah could see it from all the way across the room. She didn't know how they had all missed it the first time.

She went to take another sip and realized she had gone through the whole drink. She grimaced. Time to switch to water for a bit.

Savannah headed into the kitchen. She just picked up a glass of water when she turned to see Lucas standing at the back door. He tilted his head toward the French double doors in invitation and then sidled out of them.

She chewed on her lip. Should she go out there? Anytime she'd ever followed Lucas out to a secluded location, it had been a bad idea. Yet Liz's words were ringing in her ears. Maybe it was time to finally close that door.

With a sigh, she set her water back down and exited her parents' house. It was a beautiful North Carolina spring day. Sunny with a light breeze. Not too hot, not too humid. Just perfect. She would miss days like this when she was in DC full-time. Nothing compared to a Carolina day. She wouldn't believe anyone who told her otherwise.

Savannah found Lucas sitting on the wooden porch swing at one end of the wraparound porch. Her heels clicked on the wood as she moved over to where he was sitting. Where they had sat countless times before this moment.

He patted the seat next to him, but she remained standing. She turned her gaze off into the distance. What was she doing out here anyway?

"Savi, have a seat," Lucas said.

"Probably not a good idea."

"I wanted to give you your graduation gift."

She tilted her head up and closed her eyes. "I don't want anything."

"I know. I didn't get you something that you want."

"What?" she asked in surprise. Her dark eyes finding his baby blues.

He patted the chair again. "Sit."

"Under protest," she said, pointing her finger at him.

He just smirked. She sat.

The chair rocked back and forth a few times before either of them spoke again. It felt like déjà vu, sitting here like this. Too many memories. All those happy thoughts laced with the poison of the last four years.

Lucas reached for a wrapped box sitting next to him and then handed them to Savannah. "Here."

"What is it?"

"Just open it."

"Lucas…"

"Savi…"

He stared deeply into her eyes, and she broke contact first. She peeled backed the wrapping paper and found a small, rectangular red frame. Inside was a ticket stub to the play *Seven Brides for Seven Brothers* that she'd performed the lead in in high school. And next to it was a picture of them from that night. His arm was slung over her shoulders. She was holding an enormous bouquet of flowers that he'd brought for her. They'd been best friends then and nothing more. Easier times.

"I can't put this up in my apartment," she finally told him.

"Sure you can."

"I'm moving in with Easton." Her words were deliberate, and she made sure to make eye contact when she said them. "We've been together for three years. After all those bad summers, Lucas, I just… can't."

"You're moving in together?" Lucas demanded.

His normal chill had evaporated. She could see his frustration etched in every line.

"What do you expect me to do, Lucas?" she

asked, just as frustrated. "Wait for you? All the good that did me."

"What do you even like about that guy?"

"No," she spat. "I am not doing this with you." She shoved present back toward him. "You already know where we stand. The same place we stood that night on the beach last summer."

He gritted his teeth. "That was different."

"Don't even try."

She moved to stand up, but he placed his hand on her elbow.

"Please."

"What? What more could you want from me?"

His eyes had lost their anger. Their fire. Instead, all she saw was the adoration he'd always had for her.

"Everything."

"Stop. Please. This is never happening."

"You don't mean that."

"I do," she gasped out. "I really do."

He nodded slowly as if he couldn't really believe the words she was saying. "Well, I'll keep the frame then, I guess. But that was only half the gift." He reached into the box and retrieved a stack of paper that he pushed into her hands. He stood, pocketing the frame he'd made for her, and then placed a gentle kiss on her cheek. "Happy graduation, Savi."

She watched him walk away with a mix of fury, desperation, confusion, and pain. How could he elicit all of these emotions at once? Why did it feel wrong to do the right thing—what she knew was best for her?

She choked back the words to call out to him. Then, she forced herself to look down at the papers. She peeled them open where he'd folded them down the middle. Her hand flew to her heart.

Inside was an audition packet for a musical theater troupe in DC. For the production of *Seven Brides for Seven Brothers*.

2

A Whole New World

Two days later, Savannah stood outside of the little brownstone apartment she was renting with Easton in DC. It had completely unreasonable monthly payments for only one bedroom and bathroom. But it was DC. Nothing was inexpensive.

She knew it would be an adjustment. Her parents wanted her in some fancy place downtown. They probably already had it picked out for her when this inevitably fell apart. Or maybe that was just her cynicism talking.

She and Easton had both driven the five hours from Chapel Hill, and by some miracle, the moving truck was awaiting them when they arrived. Along with her mother.

"Mom," Savannah said in surprise after parking her car. "What are you doing here?"

Most of the time, Marilyn Maxwell lived in

Chapel Hill where she was a professor at the university. But anytime she had time off—and that was frequently now that she was a full professor—she would come up to DC to be with Savannah's father, Senator Jeff Maxwell.

"I wanted to see you into your first real apartment." She hugged Savannah and kissed her cheek. "You're the baby after all."

"Uh-huh," Savannah said with a sigh.

She was the youngest of three. It didn't help anything that Brady was a congressman and Clay had clerked for the Supreme Court and now ran his own law firm.

"Hello, Mrs. Maxwell," Easton said as he jogged toward them. "You look lovely."

Marilyn smiled. "Why, thank you. Why don't you two show me around?"

"Of course," Easton said.

He shot Savannah a raised eyebrow, and she just shrugged her shoulders. What could she say? Her mother was a force.

Savannah followed them up the stairs to the third floor with the movers close behind. She adjusted her long, dark ponytail and wished she'd had a moment to herself. After the long car ride, she really wanted to shower or at least change out of her shorts and tank top.

Easton unlocked the door and gestured for Marilyn to enter before him. Then, he waited at the top for Savannah. Her gaze traveled over his tall, muscular physique. Hair slightly rumpled from too many hours in the car. Eyes shining bright and lips upturned at the corners.

He stared down at her as if she were a dream come true. Her heart stuttered, and now, she *really* wished she had that moment alone. That smile had done her in the first time she met him. And it still did today.

Liz had actually been the one to set them up. He was Liz's tennis instructor, and when she met Savannah for lunch one day, Easton tagged along. He hadn't known then that she was a Maxwell. Or all the other bullshit that came with being the daughter of a politician. Just that they'd hit it off right away, and the rest was history.

It was still that charming smile, easy confidence, and God, yes, that tennis player's body that made her float up to him with a grin. He wrapped a tight arm around her waist and planted a kiss on her lips.

"Are you okay?" he asked.

"It'll be fine."

"Not what I asked."

"I'm okay. This is our new adventure, right?"

His smile broadened. "Right."

She reached down and squeezed his ass before walking into the apartment. She could hear him laughing behind her.

"So, what do you think?" Savannah asked her mom.

"It's…cozy."

"It'll be better once we have all the furniture."

"Of course, it will. Show me the bedroom?"

Savannah wandered into the only room in the back of the apartment while Easton directed the moving people around. She held her hands out to the sides. "Here it is. One bedroom."

"Are you really going to stay here, Savannah?" her mother asked tightly.

"Yes. I already had this conversation with you."

Marilyn sighed. "I know. I just want you to be safe."

"I'm safe. This area of town is really nice. We did a lot of research, and Easton's friends recommended it. It's trendy."

"I know. I know. I just worry. I'm your mother. It's allowed."

"You knew I wasn't going to change my mind."

"I know, dear. You are so like your father at times."

"I take that as a compliment," she said with a laugh, trying to ease the tension.

Her father was a senator for a reason. She and Brady had always been most like him even though she had no interest in politics.

"As you should," her mother said, affectionately touching her arm. When she smiled, Savannah sometimes forgot how overbearing her mother could be. "I'm glad to see that the place isn't as dodgy as I thought it would be. Perhaps, once you're settled in, you can have us over for dinner."

"I'd like that."

"Also, I have this for you." She held out a dark blue envelope.

Savannah frowned and took it from her. Inside was roundtrip airfare to Nashville for this upcoming weekend.

"Uh…what is this?"

"I know we haven't talked about it in a while, but this weekend is Lucas's graduation."

"No way."

"He came to yours."

"No, Mom. No." She tried to hand it back.

"I know things have been tense with Lucas. I don't know the details. I don't need to know them. Brady and Clay made it seem something dire." Her mother raised her eyebrows in question.

Savannah blew out heavily. "Lucas and I are complicated. Brady and Clay weren't wrong when they said it was something dire. It is. We are."

"You have known Lucas since you were both in diapers. It's reasonable to expect some complications."

Savannah snorted. Her mother didn't know the half of it. Not what had happened that summer after graduation. After years and years of being just friends and that one moment that had changed everything. Or the four years after when he'd been at Vanderbilt and only interested in her when she was home for the summer. Or last fucking summer when he'd gotten drunk and high and told her he *loved* her on Hilton Head Island. When he'd tried to kiss her as if all the other shit she had to deal with would just evaporate with those words and a kiss.

No. She and Lucas were far past complicated.

"The Atwoods are family. And even when you don't like family, you still stand by and support them."

"You don't get to make that decision for me. I told Lucas I didn't want him in my life anymore last weekend. Why would I then fly to his graduation?"

"Because it's the right thing to do, Savannah, and you know it. He knew there were problems between you two, and he still showed up, didn't he?"

Savannah grumbled something nonsensical under her breath and turned away from her mother. It wasn't even completely about going to graduation now. She could suffer through that. It was that her mother had insisted on her going and purchased her ticket for her without even asking!

"You showed up in person to give this to me because you knew, otherwise, I wouldn't go."

"Perhaps." Her mother smiled. "Friendships like Lucas Atwood's don't come around all that often, dear. Is it really worth throwing it all away?"

"Going to graduation won't change my relationship with Lucas."

"Then, you have no real objection to going." Her mother arched an eyebrow.

One of the movers entered the bedroom at that time. "Where do you want the bed?"

Savannah glared at her mother and then showed the man where to set up the bed. Marilyn kissed her cheek again, promised to come back to see the finished product, and then left with a slight wave of her hand.

She loved her mother to death, but sometimes, she got under her last nerve. It was as if because she was the only girl and the baby, she had to be constantly coddled. Clay was the total fuckup. Yet they didn't treat him like they were stepping on glass. It had been one of her favorite things about moving away for college even if it was just down the street. She could let her hair down.

"What's that?" Easton asked, entering the bedroom.

Savannah groaned and held it out to him. He was *not* going to like this.

He took the envelope and peered inside. His eyebrows rose high up his forehead. "You're going to Nashville this weekend?"

"My mother bought the tickets for me and is insisting that I go with my family."

"Uh…what's in Nashville?" He glanced back up

at her. She saw the minute it dawned on him. His brows furrowed, a line formed between his eyes, and his lips pursed. "Lucas?"

"It's his graduation. The Atwoods invited us."

He clenched his jaw and then released it. He held the paper out for her. She watched him take a deep breath.

"Have fun."

"I don't want to go." She sighed. "But I probably should."

"I know. It'll be fine." He kissed her temple.

"It's not fine. You don't mean that."

"Honestly, I do. Am I happy that you're going to Nashville to see Lucas? No. But I trust you and understand where this is coming from. I'd have to be a pretty big dick to tell you not to go."

"I could get you a ticket?"

"No offense, but I have no desire to go to his graduation. I'd go if you really wanted me to though."

"No," she said with a frown. "You don't have to go. I'm sorry I have to put you through this. There's no win here."

The whole thing was complicated. Sure, she could skip, but that would hurt her parents and the Atwoods, who had been nothing but kind to her her entire life. They were her second family. It would be rude. Plus, she had already cut ties with Lucas. No audition packet—however kind and heartfelt—could change that.

"It's not a win-or-lose situation. Look, why are we worrying about this right now? We just moved into our own place finally. Let's enjoy it. Noah said there's an ice cream place down the street that's great. We could go check it out when the movers are gone."

"Are you sure? I don't want this to bottle up between us."

"No bottling," he assured her. "I'm not some controlling boyfriend, demanding your time, okay?"

"Okay. I do wish that I didn't have to go."

"I know," he said, pulling her into his arms. He held her tight to him, running his hand up and down her back. "I wish that you didn't have to go either. But I'm realizing that's not the life we're going to live together."

She wanted to say that at least, in a month's time, Lucas would likely be drafted and move far, far away from them. But she knew that didn't matter. He'd been eight hours away from them in Nashville for four years and still fucked with her mind. Her mother was right. She'd never be able to escape the Atwoods. They were family, and it was something she and Easton were always going to have to deal with.

"Ice cream sounds great."

"Yeah?" he asked with another heart-melting smile.

"Definitely. And maybe a shower?" she asked with a laugh.

"That I can manage."

She kissed him again and watched as he started to unpack the boxes. Her heart was still heavy when she watched him. No matter what he said, she knew that he wasn't a hundred percent comfortable with this.

"Hey."

He glanced up from the box he'd been unpacking.

"You really don't have to worry about Lucas."

Easton didn't say a word. She could read it in his face though. He didn't believe that for a damn second.

And…she didn't blame him one bit.

3

Bad Ideas

S avannah's flight touched down at Nashville International Airport early Friday morning. She clutched her second coffee for the day and headed out of the terminal with her oversize purse and a rolling carry-on.

She was still not happy about this whole thing.

And she had no idea why she hadn't just told her mother to fuck off.

She didn't need to be here. She didn't need to see Lucas graduate. She loved the Atwoods, but when was she going to finally stand up and say enough was enough? Soon. Very soon.

Leaving Easton in DC their first weekend moving in together wasn't her idea of a good time. They'd had an excellent couple of days together, exploring the city and breaking the apartment in, but it had ended too quickly. Monday morning, she would start her new job, and she knew that she'd be super busy. She was really kicking herself for this.

After she exited out to the pickup line, she tugged on her enormous sunglasses and finished her coffee. She tossed it into the nearest bin before taking out her phone to text her mom.

Where are you? Landed and waiting outside.

Before she received a response, a horn honked from the street in front of her. She peeked up, wondering who the hell was being so obnoxious, and found a large silver truck with its window rolled down.

Lucas Atwood waved exaggeratedly at her. "Savi, over here."

She looked up at the sky and prayed that she wouldn't kill someone this weekend.

Lucas hopped out of the cab. He raced around to the passenger side and popped open the front door. "I'll take that."

She handed him her bag without complaint. She didn't see much point. Was this her mother's doing? Was she plotting? Or was Savannah really just this unlucky?

He loaded up her bag and then swished his head to the side to swipe his hair out of his face. She still wasn't used to his hair being this short. His blue eyes were somehow bigger and brighter. His smile megawatt. How was he so happy to see her? Didn't he remember their conversation last weekend?

"Need help?" he asked.

"I got it." Then, she reached for the handle and hoisted herself up into his giant truck.

Lucas snapped the door closed behind her and returned to the driver's seat.

"By your face, I'm going to hazard a guess that no one told you I was picking you up," he said.

Savannah's phone beeped. It was a message from her mom.

Lucas is on his way. He should be there soon.

Savannah held her phone up to Lucas. Her voice was dry. "You're on your way."

He glanced at the phone and then guffawed. "Your mom, I swear."

"Tell me about it."

She leaned back against the plush seat, kicked off her flip-flops, and crossed her legs pretzel-style.

"How's DC?"

She shrugged. "Wasn't there very long before my mom sprang this trip on me."

Lucas cringed. "She means well?" It was definitely more of a question than a statement.

Savannah didn't reply. What could she say? Her mother did mean well. But Savannah was *living* with Easton. Either her mother was being nice and trying to salvage a friendship or she was playing matchmaker with Lucas's mom...again.

As much as Savannah didn't want to, she fell into an easy rhythm with Lucas. You couldn't grow up with someone your entire life and not find the quiet comfortable. He turned on his favorite radio station, and soon, they were both singing along. Twenty minutes later, they were parked outside of his apartment in Green Hills, near the Vanderbilt campus.

"Uh…this isn't the hotel," she said.

"Yeah. I have a spare room. Your mom said you were crashing with me." Then, it seemed to dawn on him. "Well, shit. Do you want me to find you a hotel?"

She ground her teeth together. "I might kill my mother."

"That seems fair. I thought it seemed strange that you were okay with this, but I figured she knew."

Savannah really needed to have a talk with her mom. Staying at Lucas's apartment was probably not smart. But, God, she was tired of arguing with her mom. She'd have to talk to her soon enough about it. Doing it right now just did not seem ideal.

"My own room?"

"Uh…yes."

"With a door and a lock?"

He chuckled. "Also yes."

"Fine. But just for tonight. Tomorrow, I'm going to move."

"All right," Lucas said, not arguing with her.

He took her bag out of the backseat and carried it into the apartment. It was decent-sized. Bigger than the apartment she shared with Easton back in DC but with all sleek, modern amenities.

"Basketball team puts us up in these. My room-mate is already gone for the semester. So, it's just us."

"Peachy," she drawled.

"Your room is second on the right. Bathroom is at the end of the hallway. Graduation is on campus tonight, but we're pretty much free until then. There's a party afterward for the basketball team if you want to join, and then I think my mom has dinner plans tomorrow. Just so…you have all the logistics down and don't feel like people are unexpectedly throwing more shit at you."

"Thanks," she muttered.

Lucas turned to walk down the hallway, presumably to his bedroom. Then, he stopped and glanced back over his shoulder. "It's really good to have you here, Savi."

She watched him walk away with an ache in her chest that she couldn't explain. It was good to be here. Even if she'd complained repeatedly about attending. Now that she was here, she was glad that she hadn't backed out.

Savannah took his advice and found the spare bedroom. The room was bare bones. Just an extra-long bed and a dresser with an alarm clock on it. She dropped her bag off, quickly unpacked her clothes to keep them from wrinkling, and then sent Easton a quick text.

Made it safe. Miss you.
Miss you too. How's the hotel?

Savannah nearly choked on the question. Yeah, telling him that she was staying with Lucas was probably not a great idea. She knew that she *should* tell, but it would just cause him undo heartache.

It's a hotel. Mom is already driving me crazy.

Sounds right. Call me later and tell me how graduation goes.

Will do. xoxo

———

SAVANNAH SPENT the rest of the day wandering around Nashville with Lucas. They didn't meet up with their families until right before graduation. She'd changed into a Carolina blue dress for the occasion. Lucas had rolled his eyes when he saw it, but she'd just shrugged. Basketball was a religion as far as she was concerned.

Lucas disappeared to take his seat in front of the stage.

"Have fun?" her mother asked as they were walking into the alumni lawn together.

"Oodles."

Her mother shot her a skeptical look, but Savannah kept her face forward.

They found their reserved seats next to the Atwoods. Lucas's older brother, Chris, sat next to Brady and Clay. His younger sister, Alice, had her hair dyed black and swept across her forehead in a way that screamed emo. She stared down at her phone the entire time. Savannah's father took the seat next to Lucas's parents, and then Savannah sat next to her mother.

Before the ceremony got started, Savannah put her hand on her mother's shoulder. She faced Savannah in surprise.

"Don't ever do this again," she told her mother. "You may not believe that I'm an adult, but I can make my own decisions. I don't appreciate you forcing me to be here or forcing me to stay with Lucas. If you want me to do something, ask me. Don't make me. I'm not going to put up with it any longer."

Whatever Marilyn saw in Savannah's eyes must have said how serious she was because she simply nodded and turned back to face front.

That was good enough for her.

Everyone finally quieted down as the ceremony began. The sun slowly fell behind them as each student walked across the stage and had their name formally called. When the announcer said Lucas Atwood, it wasn't just their family who screamed in excitement. It was basically the entire student body. Long speeches and cheers and hats thrown, and then suddenly, it was over.

It was probably another half hour before Savannah located Lucas on the lawn amid an array of friends or possibly fans. He was taking pictures with about a dozen pretty girls. She rolled her eyes at the show and crossed her arms. Typical.

When he saw her though, a smile jumped onto his face, and he waved her over.

"Your family is looking for you," she said. "They sent me to hunt you down."

"Sorry, kind of got held up."

"Lucas, one more picture?" a girl asked, thrusting her phone in Savannah's direction.

She bobbled it in her hands and narrowed her eyes.

"Do you mind?" Lucas asked politely.

"Sure." Savannah quickly snapped the shot and handed the phone back to the girl.

"See you at the party tonight!" the girl said with big doe eyes.

"Well, that was subtle," Savannah muttered as they finally disappeared through the crowd, back toward their families.

"Tell me about it. That kind of shit happens all the time. It's exhausting."

"I'm sure it is," she said on a laugh. "Having pretty girls fawn all over you. How horrible!"

"Is that jealousy, Savannah Maxwell?"

"Hardly."

He grinned and pinched her side. "Don't worry. You're still my girl."

She opened her mouth to disagree with him, but by then, they were back with their families, and

K.A. LINDE

everyone was congratulating him. Pictures came next. His mother insisted on individuals and group shots of him in his cap and gown. After she was pushed into a picture with him, she carefully stepped out of the way and allowed the family to do their thing.

And then she just watched him.

His easy smile. His short curls. The way those blue eyes lit up around his family. The sheer size of him.

For a second, just a split second, she wished that they hadn't ruined everything four years ago. That things were easier between them. That she could forget the taste of his lips…and just have her best friend back.

4

Champagne for My Real Friends

"Are you sure I should even come with you to this party?" Savannah called down the hallway. She'd changed into a white romper that made her tan legs look like they went on for days. She sat on the edge of the bed and strapped on her nude wedges.

"Yes," he called back.

"But it's for the basketball team."

She stood from the bed just as Lucas walked in, looking all exasperated. Then, he got a glimpse of her. He stared at her with his jaw unhinged.

"Uh...do I look okay?" She pulled her long, dark hair over one shoulder.

"Maybe you shouldn't go."

"Wait, what? You were the one who told me to go to this thing. Now, you're uninviting me? Dick move."

"Every person at the party is going to hit on you."

She puffed out a breath. "Shut up. No, they won't."

"I'm going to have to keep you close tonight."

"What does that even mean?"

"Anyone with eyes can see that you're beautiful."

"Oh." She shrugged away his words. "I think more people will be interested in you anyway. So, we're good."

He arched his eyebrow. "Want to bet?"

"You're Lucas Atwood. If basketball is anything like it is at UNC, then I don't have to bet with you to know I'll win."

"I'll bet you a kiss."

"Ha! You are not getting that!"

"And here I thought, you were going to win."

She shook her head. "Nice try. But no. I don't bet my kisses."

He grinned. "Come on. Let's go."

She pushed past him down into the hallway and grabbed her purse. Lucas opened the door for her, and they jumped into an Uber to the house party about five minutes away. The house was massive and already filled to the brim with people. The lawn was overrun, and Savannah could hear the bass from the street.

"Oh God, I haven't been to a frat party since sophomore year," she grumbled.

"It's not a frat. The basketball team is worse," he

said, wrapping an arm around her shoulders and walking them forward across the brick walkway.

When they entered the plantation-style house, she shrugged him off of her. She didn't want to give anyone the impression that they were together. But judging by the expression on the girl's face who was walking toward them, it appeared to be too late.

"Lucas!" she cried.

She threw her arms around him. He hastily extracted himself from her grip.

"Amanda," he said with a head nod. "Have you seen Nick?"

"He's around," Amanda said. "I think by the kegs."

"Thanks," Lucas said. He grabbed Savannah's hand and then brushed past Amanda.

Savannah almost felt bad for the girl as they disappeared from her view. Almost. They meandered through the house until they came upon the kitchen. A half-dozen guys, all as tall as Lucas, stood around a group of kegs. A ton of other girls congregated around them, drinking out of red Solo cups and flirting outrageously with the guys.

When they saw Lucas, they all cheered.

"Lucas!"

"My man!"

One guy slapped his hand, fist-bumped, and then tapped chests. "Hey, bro. This your girl?"

"This is Savannah," Lucas said. "Savi, this is Nick."

"Hi," she said uncertainly.

Nick was looking at her as if he'd seen her before or possibly like he was going to have her for dinner.

"Savannah, Savannah," Nick said, taking her hand and kissing it. "Such a pleasure to finally meet your fine ass."

Lucas smacked the back of his head. "Watch it."

"What have you been saying about me, Lucas?" Savannah asked as she snatched her hand back.

"Nothing."

Nick crowed with laughter, tipping back his black braids. "Boy is in puppy love. I told him I'd tap that if he didn't."

Nick then wrapped an arm around her waist and carefully meandered her through the crowd of basketball players. Her head was spinning a bit. She was surprised to hear that Lucas had been talking about her. Let alone to a degree that other people already knew who she was.

A red Solo cup was pushed into her hand. She glanced down at the red drink filled with fruit and knew this was a bad idea. She should probably hand the drink back and catch an Uber to her parents' hotel. That would be smart and safe and the right thing to do.

"Don't just stare at it. Drink!" Nick said with a laugh.

Lucas put his hand on her bare back. "You don't have to if you don't want to."

"Bitch, let her have a drink." Nick pushed Lucas back. "Don't worry. I'll take care of her for you."

Savannah laughed, taking a sip of the drink and cringing. "You're outrageous. I don't think I've ever heard anyone call Lucas a bitch."

"He's a bitch if he doesn't tell me who he has meetings with next week."

"Meetings?" Savannah arched an eyebrow.

"Yeah. Teams want to meet with me and invite me out for a workout," Lucas said all nonchalant.

"For the draft?"

Lucas nodded.

"You haven't been filling her in?" Nick asked. "Lucas here is going to go big, *big*! And next year, when I go out, I'm going to go bigger. Though I already am bigger, if you know what I'm saying." Nick winked at her.

Savannah snorted. "Oh, I'm sure."

"Disbelief!" Nick cried, putting his hand to his heart. "You wound me, baby girl. You wound me."

"So…how big?" Savannah asked Lucas. When his eyes widened as if to say *don't you already know that*, she coughed and took a large gulp of her drink. "I mean, basketball!"

Lucas shrugged dismissively. "We'll see next week. Utah, LA, and Oklahoma City asked for meetings."

"Fucking hell, LA?" Nick groaned. "I hate you."

"Nothing is set in stone."

"Wow," Savannah said softly. "Those are all... really far away."

"Aren't you a reporter?" Nick asked.

She nodded. God, he really did know a shit-ton about her.

"Well, should be easy to get a job wherever he ends up."

Savannah nearly spit out her drink. "First, that's not how reporting jobs work *at all*. Second, why the hell would I move with him?"

Lucas was cracking up laughing. His face was buried in his beer.

"I thought this was happening." Nick pointed between Lucas and Savannah.

"Nope. I have a boyfriend in DC. This," she said, gesturing between herself and Lucas, "is not happening."

"Well, shit. Where's little ole boyfriend now?"

"Home."

"Uh-huh." Nick sounded disbelieving.

"Lay off, Nick. It's amazing she agreed to come to the party. Let's just chill and have a good time," Lucas said.

"Whatever you say, bro."

Savannah fell into step with Lucas's friends. Mostly basketball players and the occasional girl. Amanda kept showing up and trying to throw herself at Lucas, but he kept trying to push her off on Nick.

Savannah was pretty sure that Nick was all right with that.

They moved into the sitting area. A DJ had been set up, and people were dancing. Savannah was deep into her third glass of punch. She had known she should stop after one, but it didn't even taste like alcohol. Which was how she should have known not to drink it.

"What…is in this?" she asked, stumbling forward into Lucas.

"How much have you had?" he asked.

Savannah held up three fingers. "And a pineapple. It was so yum."

Lucas laughed. "Maybe we should get you water. That has Everclear in it."

"Fuck," she mumbled. "I might be drunk."

Lucas took the drink out of her hand and dropped it off on a nearby table. "Water."

"I'm fine." She grabbed his hand. "Let's dance."

"Sav."

"Oh my God, this song!" she cried.

Just then "Get Low" came on, and everyone yelled at the same time, "Win-dowwwww!"

Lucas laughed. "Do you remember how we used to all dance to this in high school?"

"And I had no idea what skeet was."

"Such an innocent, Maxwell."

"I'll show you innocent," she snapped.

She grabbed the cup he'd set down and downed

the rest of the contents. Then, with his hand in hers, she veered them out into the crowd. Lucas made no protest. Shocking.

Their bodies twined together in the packed, heated crowd. With loose summer clothing exposing so much skin and sweat beading on foreheads and the music driving everyone along, it was a perfect atmosphere. Lucas's hands were on her hips. She had hers overhead. Their hips were locked and swayed provocatively. They moved as one unit. As if this were natural. As if they'd done this before. Time and time again.

Someone bumped into her from behind, and she dropped her arms around his neck, giggling. His lips were dangerously close. Inches away. It would be so easy to forget where she was and what she was doing, but she hadn't had that much to drink. Her heart beat against her rib cage, and Lucas leaned forward and rested his forehead against hers.

"God, I want to kiss you," he said over the bass.

"I...can't."

"I know."

With a racing heart, she turned away from the temptation of his lips. Not that it made it much better when her ass was pressed up against his dick. Not when it was clear from that position *exactly* what he wanted. And kissing was only the beginning.

She quieted her mind—or the alcohol did—and she pretended like this was any other night. Any other time. Nothing to worry about. She could handle this. She was a big girl.

Then, the whole crowd yelled to touch her toes, and she was drunk enough to do it. Her fingers touching the tops of her wedges. One of his hands splayed on the base of her spine. The other gripped her hip and pulled her closer. She ran her hands up her legs and flipped her hair.

He pulled her back in again, and she read the word he mouthed, *Fuck*.

"Maybe...maybe another drink," she said and then pushed herself out of the dance floor.

She knew he was following her, but she didn't care. She just wanted to not think about it. About him. She needed to think about her boyfriend at home in DC. The one she loved and who trusted her. The one she hadn't called after graduation like planned.

Goddamn it! Well, it'd have to wait until morning.

She needed another drink to think about how *that* conversation was going to go. She downed a fourth glass of punch before Lucas reached for the cup.

"Maybe you should slow down," Lucas said.

"Why?" She turned away from him and asked for another.

"Savannah."

"Lucas."

"Fine. I'll hold your hair back later or whatever."

"Ew. No way."

It was somewhere between glass five and twenty… in the middle of which she'd lost count. She forgot why she should be worried about tonight. She forgot why she hadn't wanted to be here. She even forgot that she hadn't even liked this girl Amanda earlier today. Now, they were obviously best friends. Lifelong friends for sure. Roughly five hundred pictures, a chorus of "Girls Just Want to Have Fun," and dancing on a table outside later, and she decided her night had been epic.

Lucas, of course, was never too far away. He'd caught her when she almost fell off the table and laughed at their terrible rendition of Cyndi Lauper. He'd probably taken half of the pictures that weren't selfies. But mostly, he'd just watched her get sloshed with an amused expression on his face.

"What?" she asked in the wee hours of the morning when everything was finally winding down.

"I haven't seen you like this in a long time."

"I have fun," she said, smacking him in the chest.

"Usually, you're so angry with me."

She curled her fingers into his T-shirt. "Why would I be angry with you?"

Lucas laughed. "Now, that is a can of worms."

"Don't condescend to me," she slurred.

"Big words for someone as wasted as you."

"I am…n-not wasted."

Then, he was laughing even harder. "Maybe we should get you home. Party is basically over."

She skipped past him toward the entrance once more, and he basically ran to catch up with her as he called for an Uber. She stumbled, nearly falling face-first, and that was about the point where he hauled her into his arms and carried her through the house. The Uber arrived a couple of minutes later.

"She'd better not throw up in here," the Uber driver said.

"She won't," Lucas said. He eased her into the backseat, and she leaned her head against the window to watch the streetlights. "She hates throwing up."

"I really, *really* do."

When they got back to his apartment, he put an arm around her to help her into his place. "You know, Savi, it's a good thing you didn't bet," he muttered as he opened the door for her.

"Bet?"

"Our kiss."

"Mmm…"

"I would have definitely won." He closed the door.

She shook her head. "No, everyone wants you."

"Blatantly false. I had to hover over you all night to keep the creeps away."

"You did not!" She smacked him again playfully in disbelief and then nearly fell over.

He shook his head and then scooped her up into his arms. She sighed and rested her head on his chest as he carried her into the guest bedroom. He set her down on the bed and then carefully removed each of her shoes, tossing them to the side.

She stood on wobbly feet. He completely towered over her without the shoes. God, he was so tall.

"You should try to sleep this off," he suggested.

"Will you help me out of this?" She twirled around and pointed at the zipper on the back.

"I…" She could hear him audibly gulp. "Let me get you a change of clothes."

He snagged the zipper and then hastily retreated to her suitcase. He found shorts and a T-shirt and tried to blindly hand them to her. She slipped the T-shirt over her head and let the romper fall to the ground. She couldn't be bothered with the shorts. That sounded like effort.

"Are you ready?"

"Uh-huh."

He turned around, and his eyes went straight to her legs. "Shorts?"

"Nah." She reached out for him and drew him down onto the bed with her. "You sleep here now."

"Savi, you're drunk."

"Nope." She curled her body into his and let the room spin all around her.

"Sav…"

She tilted her head up to look at him, and he stopped talking. That energy that had coursed between them on the dance floor ignited once more.

She slipped her hand up into his curls, running her fingers through them.

"Scared?" she murmured.

Then, his lips were on hers, crushing her, tasting her, needing her. A desperate, feverish kiss. Passion and aching and yearning all rolled up into one touch. His bulk pressed her back into the bed, carefully leaning on top of her. The shirt she was wearing bunched up to her stomach. She hooked a leg around him, trying to get him closer, needing this like she'd never needed anything.

His hands explored, running up into her hair, over her neck, down her sides. All while their tongues melded together. Their bodies rocking in a motion that was all too familiar.

"Oh God," she moaned as he started kissing down her neck.

A hand snaked up her T-shirt. He traced the outline of her breast, teased her pert nipple, and then cupped it fully. Her back arched off of the bed. Her body demanding more, more, more. Her brain on rapid fire.

"Please," she whispered.

Then, suddenly, Lucas was gone. He was standing a foot away from her. His chest heaving. His eyes dilated. His erection very, very evident.

"Wha…"

"You…don't want this," he finally said. "And I'm not going to have you hate me in the morning because I took advantage of you when you were drunk. If you want me, then you want me sober. A week ago, you could hardly look at me. I know this isn't right. I knew, and I kissed you anyway. Fuck. But I want you."

"Lucas," she whispered.

He turned away, cursing under his breath. "Go to sleep, Savannah."

Then, he marched out the door and slammed it shut behind him.

She blacked out before he was even back in his own room.

5

Whoops

"Shut. Up," Savannah groaned.

She reached out and slammed her hand down on her cell phone, trying to cease the insistent buzzing noise coming from the nightstand. She cracked an eye open and winced at the blast of sunlight. Her head was the size of a watermelon, and any minute, it was going to split open.

For a brief second, the noise cut off. She sighed and rested back. She wanted to go back to sleep for another century or two.

She wasn't that lucky.

The buzzing started again. She grabbed her phone and brought it close to her face. She saw through slit eyelids that Easton was calling. Oh, this wasn't going to be fun.

"Hello?" she asked groggily.

"Savannah, fuck," Easton growled into the phone.

She tugged it a bit farther from her ear. "Can you keep it down? My head is throbbing."

"Keep it down?" His voice was sharp.

"Please."

"I've been calling you for hours. It's one in the afternoon, and you just answered your phone. I didn't know if you were dead or what the fuck had happened after seeing your social media blow up all night long."

"What's blowing up? I've been asleep."

A harsh breath pushed into the phone. Easton was pissed off. That was what that breath meant. She needed to get her head on and figure out what he was pissed about. Slowly, she eased into a sitting position, which didn't help her head, but was better than nothing.

"Easton?"

"What did you do last night, Savannah?" he finally asked.

"Oh," she muttered. She put her head in her hand. Well, that wasn't how she wanted to have this conversation. "I went to a graduation party for the basketball team."

"Yeah. I think the entire world knows that by now."

"It was nothing, Easton. I should have told you, but we just had a few drinks and then came home."

Or at least…that was about all that she remembered. How exactly *had* she gotten back here last night?

"Well, your new best friend, Amanda, posted pictures of you together. Remember those?"

Fuck…she didn't.

"Uh…"

Easton let loose another breath. "Great."

"I mean…I didn't know she was posting the pictures." She only briefly remembered that she'd taken pictures with Amanda. She was also pretty sure she hadn't liked Amanda at the beginning of the night.

"Just tell me…would you have even told me about you and Lucas if someone else hadn't posted pictures?"

Her heart started to race. What the fuck *had* Amanda posted last night? She put Easton on speakerphone and started scrolling through her social media. There were dozens of pictures. She and Amanda dancing on tables, taking shots, watching the guys do keg stands. She and Lucas standing close together, one of them dancing together, one of them laughing about who the fuck knew what, smiling up at each other, and on and on. So many fucking pictures. Well, shit.

"I…yes," she finally said. "I was going to tell you this morning that I had gone with him. But these pictures, they look bad…but nothing happened."

"What would you think if you saw this and I didn't answer?"

She tilted her head to the sky. "I'd think the worst."

"Yeah."

She chewed on her bottom lip. "It's really not what it looks like."

"I want to believe that."

"We were just hanging out. There's nothing between me and Lucas."

"I'm pretty sure he doesn't agree with you."

"Well, his opinion doesn't matter."

Easton sighed. She could practically see him rubbing a hand down his face. "Okay."

"Okay?"

"What else am I supposed to say? I almost booked a flight to Nashville this morning. But I thought I should talk to you before I got there and put my fist through his fucking face. He knows what he's doing. That's for sure."

"It's not like that."

"I know the party line. You've known each other forever. Your parents are best friends. The Maxwell-Atwood wedding was planned in infancy."

"That's not fair," she muttered. This was doing nothing for her headache. "That's not how I feel, and you know it."

"You're right," he said on another sigh. "It's not

what you want, but that's how the pictures were painted."

"I'm sorry that I put you in that position."

"Just come home soon, okay?"

"As soon as I can."

"I love you, Savannah."

She smiled. "I love you too."

As soon as Easton hung up, Savannah jumped out of bed. Holding her aching head, she threw open her door and stomped down the hallway to Lucas's bedroom. She didn't even bother knocking on the door, just stormed right inside.

"Lucas Nathaniel Atwood," she yelled.

The shower turned off, and a second later, Lucas appeared in the doorway, wearing nothing but a white towel and a shit-eating grin. "Can I help you, Savi?"

"First, put some fucking clothes on, and second, what the fuck happened last night?"

Lucas flipped his wet hair out of his eyes. Savannah was careful not to let her eyes drift any lower to the sculpted body below. To the built chest or the six-pack abs or the V peeking out of the top of the towel. Her eyes snapped back up. Focus.

"You're the one only wearing a T-shirt," Lucas pointed out.

Savannah's gaze dropped to her bare legs. Jesus Christ, how the hell had she gotten into this position? She tugged her shirt down lower to cover more of her thighs. "Ugh! How did I even get into this T-shirt?"

Lucas walked over to a drawer and tossed basketball shorts at her. She caught them and quickly slipped into them, rolling them down about ten times so they fit her.

"You really don't remember?"

She shook her head once.

"Fuck," he groaned.

"I need to know what happened. There are pictures of us together all over the internet, Lucas. Your friend Amanda is a real peach."

The smile slid off of his face. "What's the last thing you remember?"

Her cheeks heated. "We were dancing at the party. Then, I had another drink, and it gets fuzzy from there."

Lucas didn't answer her. He rifled through his drawers until he pulled out a shirt, basketball shorts, and boxers. Then, he disappeared back into the bathroom for what felt like way too long just to change. Savannah tried not to tap her foot in irritation. She knew that she shouldn't have gotten that drunk. She'd put herself in this position. But damn, it'd be great if Lucas filled her.

The man who stepped back out of that bathroom was a different person than the one who had walked in. Gone were the easy smiles and playful demeanor. He looked serious and irritated.

"What?" she asked. Fear struck her. "Did…something happen?"

Lucas didn't look at her as he shook his head.

"Lucas?" she whispered.

"The one time I'm a good person, and you don't even remember."

Savannah swallowed. "What does that mean?"

Lucas looked her in the eyes. "Nothing happened, Savannah. Go home to your boyfriend."

He brushed past her and out of his room. She felt tears pricking at her eyes, and she couldn't even explain them. She didn't want something to have happened. But the way he'd said it...it sounded so hopeless. Like something could have happened, but it didn't because of him and not her. Her stomach turned.

She'd had no expectations for this weekend. If anything, she thought that she would watch him graduate and get out of there as soon as possible. At best, she hoped that they could get their friendship back on track. Even that had seemed unrealistic after what they'd been through. Now, here she was, thinking that she had somehow made it worse and she didn't even know how.

She brushed a hand under her eyes and followed after him. She found him in the kitchen, brewing coffee. "Come on, Lucas. We should talk about this."

"There's nothing to talk about," he said with his back to her.

"I thought you wanted to fix this. I was dragged here for your graduation. You can at least have the decency to explain to me what happened last night. I don't want to walk away this weekend with us on bad terms. We've been friends for so long."

Lucas whipped around. "We're not friends!" he roared.

Savannah took a shocked step backward.

"We haven't been friends for years, Savi! We grew up together and have been one step away from fucking since high school. That's what we are," he spat. "We went different ways. You chose North Carolina. I chose Vanderbilt. We come together every summer, get fucked up, and fuck. You feel guilty about it. You get pissed at me. You blame me. But this is what we are. I don't know when you're going to see that."

She swallowed hard. "Fuck you, Lucas."

"Yeah, I probably should have. At least you'd have a real reason to feel guilty when you run back to him. Again."

"God, I don't even know why I bother." She shook her head. "You've led me on for years with your bull-shit. I should have seen through you long ago."

"Whatever lie you have to tell yourself."

"Lie?" she nearly shrieked.

"Who led who on, Savi? You dated every other guy in high school other than me."

"So, what? You're punishing me for not fucking you in high school?"

"I'm not fucking punishing you. I'm telling you

the truth you don't want to hear." He stepped forward until they were nearly touching. His breath hot on her face. "When you're drunk, all you want is me inside you, and when you're sober, all you do is try to convince yourself that isn't true."

Savannah narrowed her eyes. "You're full of shit."

"So, if you want to fuck right now, then I'm all for it. Otherwise, get out of my face," he snarled.

"I hate you."

"Good."

"I'm leaving!"

"Even better."

Savannah wanted to scream as she stalked back to the room she'd been staying in. She threw all of her stuff back into her suitcase and hurtled toward the door. "Thanks for proving time and time again why we never fucking work."

"Right back at you, babe."

She glared at him once more before walking through the front door and slamming it in his douchebag face.

6

Early Bird Gets the Worm

Savannah took a deep breath and then turned the key in the lock. Before the door was all the way open, she could see Easton had jumped up from where he was seated on the couch among several stacks of papers. A rerun of *West Wing* was playing in the background. His hair was mussed, as if he'd been running his fingers through it all afternoon. He had two days' worth of growth along his jawline and circles under his eyes. Still, he looked like home.

"Savannah?"

"Hey," she said, pushing her suitcase into the living room.

"You're not supposed to be home until tomorrow."

"I know. I changed my flight." She shut the door behind her and dropped her purse on the floor. "I never should have left. I missed you."

She crossed the small room and threw her arms around his neck. He pulled her close, breathing in her scent. This was what she needed. Just to feel his arms holding her and their hearts beating as one.

"I missed you too," he murmured against her cheek.

"I'm sorry about this weekend, Easton," her voice broke.

She was still so upset about Lucas and their fight. So mad that she'd let him get under her skin. Why should he have that kind of power? She should have been here with Easton, where she was happy. Not being stupid with Lucas.

He wasn't wrong. They were constantly on a precipice that felt precarious at best. Like she was going to free fall at every turn. And it wasn't good for her. It never had been. This, this right here, was what she wanted.

"Shh," Easton said. "You don't have anything to apologize for."

"You didn't want me to go. We both knew it wasn't a good idea, and I did it anyway."

He brushed a strand of her hair behind her ear. "That wasn't you. That was your parents. You can't blame yourself."

"Yeah, but then the party and the pictures. I know it looked bad."

"That did look bad," he agreed. "I can admit I

was worried. And I wish you had just been honest with me about going."

"I know. I should have. I don't know why I didn't tell you, and I definitely didn't think I'd drink that much."

"Look, if nothing happened and you just had a lot to drink, then it doesn't matter. Okay?" he said, his voice so earnest.

There was so much she wanted to say to that. How guilty she felt. How she should have the blame. And it did matter. The more she thought about last night, the more pieces seemed to filter through her brain. Lucas had said nothing had happened, but... had it? Why did she remember asking if he was scared? And what did that mean?

The fact that she didn't know made it worse. Because...she could have done *anything* with him and not know. That wasn't right. Let alone healthy. It certainly wasn't how she wanted her relationship with Easton to be. She'd flip her shit if it were the other way around. So, why was it any different when it came to her and Lucas?

It wasn't any different. Lucas had been coming between them long enough. She needed to keep that door closed. For good.

"I know, but..." she began.

"It's behind us," he insisted. "Let's just move forward. That's what this move was about, right?"

"Right," she whispered.

His lips landed on hers, soft and inviting. A gentle coax to open her mouth and let him in. Let him back into her heart.

She leaned into him, feeling the gentle caress and the ease with which she landed in his arms again. His strong tennis arms that circled her, claimed her.

Whatever had happened this weekend was over. She needed to be in the here and now. Present. When she was with Easton, it was so easy. Effortless.

His hands slid down her back, over her ass, and down to her thighs. He hoisted her into the air and wrapped her legs around his waist. She held on to him as he walked them back into their bedroom. The one that definitely needed to be broken in again.

———

MONDAY MORNING DAWNED bright and early. Nerves pricked at Savannah as she took the Metro to the K Street stop and exited into the sunshine that brightened Franklin Square. She took a deep breath to calm herself and followed the crowd toward the gold revolving doors of *The Washington Post*.

It felt surreal to walk across the black-and-white tiled floor and see the high marbled walls all around her. She'd dreamed of this moment for so long. Reporting had been her goal from a young age. Even when people tried to push her to news broadcasting, claiming her pretty face should be on a television screen, she'd been enamored with newspapers. She'd read them religiously, growing up, and she refused to believe that they were a dying market.

She crossed to the row of brass elevators and followed the instructions she had been emailed last week. She stepped out of the elevator with ten other people who all clearly knew where they were going. Savannah glanced down at the email once more and turned a circle.

"Newbie?"

She turned to see a woman with shoulder-length, curly brown hair and full red lips. She wore black pants, a floral blouse, and stiletto red pumps.

"Uh…yes. That obvious?"

"Always." She held her hand out. "Dylan Gonzalez."

Savannah took it. "Savannah Maxwell."

"Ohhh," Dylan said, dragging the word out. "The Maxwell chick. Yeah, I've heard of you."

Savannah grimaced. Great, her name had preceded her. "Oh dear."

Dylan laughed. "Come on. I think you're McAllister's assistant. He's a hard-ass and way old school. Good luck with that."

"I'm up to the challenge."

"That's what the last three said. He kind of rides you into the ground." Dylan contemplatively pressed a finger to her lips. "Metaphorically, of course."

"I'd hope so."

Dylan snickered. "Definitely." She knocked twice on a large corner office. "McAllister, your new girl is here."

"Send her in."

Dylan squeezed her shoulder once reassuringly. "Give 'em hell, Maxwell."

Savannah stepped forward into her boss's office. He was a tall, fit man with pale skin and a slightly receding hair line. He looked like the kind of guy who used to play football in high school and hadn't quite let himself go. He shot her a blank look and absent-mindedly gestured around his office.

"Miss Maxwell, come in. I'm Rich McAllister."

She stepped in carefully. "Nice to meet you, sir."

"Your office is the cubicle across from mine. Mitch can help you set up. I like my coffee with cream and two sugars, and I like them regularly." He waved his hand again. "Welcome to the team."

Savannah opened her mouth to respond, but he had already turned back to his computer. So much for making a great first impression.

Mitch had the cubicle next to her and sighed when he saw her. "Maxwell?"

"Yes. Savannah."

"Great. I like my coffee with hazelnut creamer and two Splenda packets," he told her. "Just throw your stuff down and head over to the coffee station, stat."

"Oh…okay."

Halfway to the coffee station, she took two more orders. She tried not to curse anyone as she made all the drinks as best and fast as she could. She put them in a carrier. But when she wound back through the cubicles, she found the office empty.

"What the hell?" she mumbled.

Then, she saw the conference room. Great.

She eased the door open with her toe and came in to a spatter of laughter. Everyone was looking at *her* and laughing. Her cheeks bloomed red, and she tried to cover it by walking forward to pass out coffee.

"You're late for the morning meeting," McAllister said. "Hurry and pass that out and take your seat."

She gulped and hastily handed everyone coffee. Then, she dropped into the nearest seat and pulled a notebook toward her. She took notes through the entire meeting but was back on coffee duty by the afternoon.

While she was sinking halfway under an ever-growing pile of paperwork that had materialized on her last coffee run, a familiar face appeared.

"Hey Maxwell, ready to quit yet?" Dylan asked.

Savannah grinned. "No way."

"They make you get coffee all day?"

She nodded.

"Yeah, sounds right. It'll get better. They just don't think you're qualified."

Savannah's eyes rounded. "Uh, why?"

"Because you're a Maxwell. Everyone thinks daddy got you this job," Dylan told her.

"Why are you telling me this?"

Dylan shrugged and leaned against her cubicle. "Why not? No one else is honest. And if it's true, then you'll scrub out in a couple of weeks anyway. If it's not, maybe you'll prove everyone wrong."

Savannah glanced back at the stack of paperwork. This wasn't what she wanted to be doing. But everyone had to start somewhere.

"You think my dad would have gotten me a position where I had to get everyone coffee?" she asked with a smirk. "If he had it his way, I'd have McAllister's job already."

Dylan snorted. "I like you. Let's get drinks sometime."

"Done."

"Maybe after you crawl your way out of that hole," Dylan said, pointing at the stack of paperwork.

"Yeah…no kidding."

"I'll be waiting," Dylan said. She fluttered her fingers in Savannah's direction as she departed.

"Me too," Savannah muttered under her breath.

Savannah stayed well past close. It was a couple of hours later when she pulled herself out of the paperwork long enough to see the time and that she had missed several calls from Easton.

She called him back. "Hey, so sorry I didn't answer. I've been swamped."

Easton laughed on the other line. "I was actually calling because I'm still at the office."

"Oh," she said with a laugh. "Well, at least we're on the same schedule."

"Pretty much. Brady wants me to go back to North Carolina with him this weekend."

"Ugh! Already?"

"I ran that office for him. It's good for me to travel with him."

"Yeah, yeah," she grumbled.

"Maybe you should see Liz while I'm gone. I know you two haven't gotten a chance to catch up."

"That's actually a great idea."

"See you at home later?"

Savannah grinned. "I'll leave a spot for you in bed."

"Don't steal all the covers."

"Psh," she muttered. "As if that's me."

Easton laughed. "That's absolutely you, love."

"Fine. Just try not to wake me up when you come in."

She could practically see Easton's wolfish grin through the phone. "Oh, I have every intention of waking you up."

"Don't start that with me, or I might just have to come home before I finish this paperwork."

"All right, all right. Get your work done, and I'll see you in a few hours. Love you."

"You too. Bye."

Savannah hung up the phone with a pleased smile on her face. Since she'd walked away from Lucas, things had been so good with Easton. She already felt like they were back where they were supposed to be.

Before she forgot about it, she dialed Liz's number.

Her sister-in-law answered on the second ring. "Savannah! Oh my God, I was just thinking about you."

"Well, good timing then. I hear the boys are going out of town this weekend."

"Ugh! Is Brady dragging Easton along too? I swear, they plan these things without us on purpose."

"Tell me about it," Savannah said. She leaned the phone between her head and shoulder and clicked over to the next document she was working on. "But since we have the weekend free, I was thinking we could hang out."

"I would *love* that. How about dinner Friday night? I know this Indian place downtown that is to die for. I'll make Brady get us a reservation."

"Oh God, no," Savannah said quickly. "As much as I'd love a fancy dinner, I really just want laid-back girl time and maybe a beer. I think I'm going to need one at the end of this week."

"Is it that bad?" Liz asked with concern.

Liz knew what it was like. She had been Savannah's editor at the college newspaper that they had both ended up running. But after a scandal with

Brady, she'd never fully recovered her love of journalism. Now, she was at Maryland, getting her PhD.

"You have no idea. I'll tell you all about it when I see you Friday."

"Okay. I'll pick something more low-key, and maybe we can do Rasika another night."

"Put me down for it. I can't wait to catch up."

"Me either! There's something I've been meaning to tell you."

"Bad?" Savannah asked.

"Of course not. It's nothing. We'll talk about it Friday."

"All right. If you're sure."

"Completely."

Savannah hung up the phone, but she wondered what Liz could have to talk to her about. Hopefully, it actually wasn't bad. Because she could not handle something else going wrong in her life. She surveyed the enormous pile of paperwork she had to get through with a sigh. Better get cracking.

7

Surprise, Surprise

"I hate that we keep missing each other every weekend," Easton said. He tugged Savannah closer and leaned his foreheads against hers. "One of these days, we will both be home all weekend and actually get to spend some time together."

"One day. If I ever get caught up on work."

"Don't let them intimidate you."

"Oh, I'm not intimidated," she told him. "I'm pissed. I didn't think I'd be top dog by noon or anything, but I thought someone would at least take me seriously."

"Stick with it, and someone will."

"Yeah, yeah," she said, waving her hand. "I know. That's what Dylan says too."

"I think I need to meet this Dylan. You've talked about her all week."

"Well, when she's the only person in the entire

building who is nice to you, it's easy to talk about her. Plus, she's gorgeous, funny, and brilliant."

"Maybe you should date her instead," he said with a laugh.

"Maybe I should. She speaks Spanish too." She winked at him.

"Well, that definitely beats out my tennis skills."

Savannah giggled. "You're ridiculous. Now, hurry up before you're late. Brady doesn't like to wait."

Easton grinned and pulled her in for a kiss. "Don't have too much fun with Liz. She's a troublemaker."

"Yeah, right."

"Okay, maybe that's just my imagination when I think about you two together."

She swatted him. "Oh my God, Easton!"

"A guy can dream!" he said, ducking out of her reach. "I love you. Have fun!"

She shook her head with a grin on her face and watched him leave out of their apartment. She loved that man and all of his ridiculousness. She wished that he could be here this weekend. But work always came first for both of them. At least she had Liz. It would be nice, catching up. They hadn't spent nearly enough time together since Liz had moved to DC two years ago.

Savannah checked the time. If she was going to beat traffic, she needed to head out too. Of course, beating the traffic in DC was like saying the sky was green and the grass was blue. It was always horrendous, even at odd hours. Not to mention, all the drivers were insane. She'd thought The Triangle was bad, but it was nothing compared to DC drivers.

She probably should have taken the Metro, but she didn't want to get stuck if they stayed out late. And since the place was closer to Brady and Liz's, she figured she might end up crashing there anyway. Especially since her brother was gone for the weekend.

It took a solid forty-five minutes of cussing out the traffic to get to the sports bar that they had chosen for its excellent selection of craft beer. Savannah wasn't the world's biggest beer fan, but after her week, she needed it. And maybe something stronger.

The place was crowded already when she entered. It had wall-to-wall big-screen televisions with an enormous horseshoe bar at the center. Booths lined the restaurant and high-top tables took up most of the center of the space. It was loud and a bit overwhelming. She was wondering if it would have been better to pick a quieter place, so they could chat.

But then she saw Liz at the bar and decided it didn't matter.

She hurried over to her friend and grabbed her tight.

"Look at you, all grown up," Liz said with a laugh. "I remember when we were in college, and you wouldn't even drink around the other journalists."

She held her at arm's length. "Now, you're requesting a bar for dinner."

"Ugh! I drank in college."

"Just not around us."

"Sometimes. But you know how it is. It's easy to feel like your every move is being watched."

Liz nodded. "I absolutely know that feeling. Senior year was kind of a disaster because of it. And I was just joking anyway. I'm glad you're here. I can't believe we have you, Brady, and Clay in the same city. The Maxwell siblings have arrived."

Savannah plopped down next to her. "I feel lucky. I always thought that I'd be far from my brothers. Clay has been here forever since he was working for the Supreme Court. And then Brady was elected to the House. It kind of felt inevitable that I'd end up here. But, of course, I had no idea it would be *The Washington Post*. Most journalists have to pay their dues in a small-town newspaper. I apparently have to pay them at a huge newspaper."

"Aww," Liz said sympathetically, "is it really that bad?"

"You have no idea." She shot her an exasperated look.

"Tell me about it. I was hoping that you'd have good news about the job."

"Let's get something to drink first."

Liz waved her hand at the cute bartender, who hustled over. "We'll take an order of chips and salsa.

My friend here wants a Blue Moon, and I'll just have…" She scrolled the menu and then glanced up at Savannah. "Will you kill me if I have a Coke? I'm really not feeling up to a beer."

Savannah waved her hand at Liz. "Whatever you want. I just really need a beer."

"Great. A Coke and a water with lemon."

"Got it. Coming right up." The bartender gave them both a dimpled grin and then filled their drinks.

Savannah took a large gulp of her beer. "I really, really needed that."

"Okay. What's going on?" Liz drank her Coke. "This isn't like you to be so stressed out. Actually…I don't think I've ever seen you stressed out."

"Well, I also wasn't forced to be the coffee girl for the entire department. I'm all for paying my dues. That's fine by me. But they're doing it because they think my dad got me the job, and if they push me hard enough, I'll scrub out."

"That's absurd. Why would your dad get you a job where you get everyone's coffee?" Liz asked with a laugh.

Savannah threw her hand out. "I know! That's what I said. He's a freaking senator. He has more sway than that. I got this job on my own merits. Not that anyone seems to care."

"And the boss?"

She shrugged. "He's fine. I'm filing paperwork, sending emails, and answering phone calls. I don't mind it. Being his assistant could get me another job in the department if I work my way up. And honestly, he's not even that bad. He just expects me to leave. He's had three other assistants, and they all left."

"Well, there you go. You're not going to leave. Give it some time, and he'll see that you're different."

"I just wish that my name hadn't done this to me."

"What? Open doors?" Liz asked with a chuckle.

"Make everyone hate me because I'm a Maxwell."

"Shush," Liz said, taking another long sip. "All you Maxwells are charming, confident, and hard-working."

"Even Clay?" Savannah asked. She bit down on her lip to keep from laughing.

"Especially Clay! And anyway, Brady and Clay had to prove themselves to get to where they are. You will too."

"You're right. Of course you're right. I'm just a stress ball. At least there's one person I like at work."

"That's progress."

"Yeah, her name is Dylan. I think you'd like her. She's very…blunt."

Liz snorted. "Blunt like Victoria?" she asked about her best friend from college.

"Maybe not…that blunt. But I like her. It'd be nice to have a friend. Or at least an ally."

"That it would. You should invite her to hang out with us sometime. Brady is putting together a party next weekend. She could come with you."

Savannah reached for their chips, which the cute bartender had just brought over. "I'll see if she's interested."

Even though Dylan had said that they should get drinks, Savannah hadn't thought to invite her today. Mostly, she needed a vent session. But maybe Dylan could come along to Brady's.

Actually, now that she thought about it, she should probably get drinks with Dylan solo first. Savannah's family was intimidating. And she didn't want her only friend to think that she was trying to show off or something. Savannah couldn't help but constantly be conscious of all of this. She wished she weren't, but bringing new people into the fold was always a bit more like brain surgery. It wasn't like everyone fit so seamlessly into the Maxwell family like Liz.

"No rush, ladies," the cute bartender said, swiping his brown hair out of his eyes. "But if you're ready to order…"

They both put in their orders for delicious, greasy food hamburgers with fries and onion rings and then resumed their conversation.

"And how are things with Easton?" Liz asked.

"Really good. After that fiasco last weekend, I'm glad that we're even on speaking terms."

"Fiasco?" Liz raised her eyebrows. "What did I miss?"

"My mom forced me to go to Lucas's graduation."

"Oh right."

"Yeah, and I went with him to a party for the basketball team and got shit-faced." Savannah shook her head. "Some girl at the party took all these pictures of us and posted them online. Easton woke up to them and flipped his shit."

"Understandably."

"Yeah. And I, um…screamed at Lucas and told him I hated him and never wanted to see him again. Then, I took the first flight home."

Liz blew out her breath heavily. "Well, that couldn't have gone worse."

"I know. Easton and I are fine now. I apologized and everything because it was stupid. But is it bad to feel…guilty about what I said to Lucas?"

Savannah bit her lip. She hadn't even let herself think that this last week. But she could say anything to Liz. She had been there through almost all of it with Lucas.

"I don't know, Savi. He's your best friend, and you two have history. I don't blame you for getting upset with him though. But if you feel guilty, then maybe Easton isn't the only one you should apologize to."

"Ugh!" she groaned. "I'm just so mad at him. He drives me crazy."

"Yeah. That's because you love him."

Savannah whipped her head to the side. "I do not love him!"

Liz's laughter bubbled out of her, and she put her

hand on Savannah's shoulder. "You always have. Even if just as a friend."

"He's so infuriating."

"It's because he's known you your entire life, so he can push all your buttons."

"I wish he'd stop," she mumbled under her breath. Savannah sighed and drained the rest of her beer. "Okay, let's stop talking about me. I'm a freaking Greek tragedy right now. What did you want to tell me?"

"Well…" Liz said, straightening. A giant smile spread on her face, and she bit her lip. "I wanted to tell you in person, and I haven't seen you yet, so…I'm pregnant."

"Oh my God!" Savannah shrieked. She hopped off of her barstool and jumped up and down. "You're pregnant. Oh my God! Liz!"

She squealed and threw her arms around her sister-in-law and closest friend. She couldn't believe this. It was so magical.

"You're going to be an aunt," Liz told her.

"When did you find out? Tell me everything."

"It's only been a couple of weeks. We don't know much yet, except that I'm due January 31st."

"That's incredible. Are you going to stay in school?"

Liz nodded. "Yep. I worked it out with the department so that I could finish next semester. I'll take a semester off for the baby and then come back to finish my third year in the fall."

"That's…wow. I am so happy for you. Is Brady over the moon?"

"You have no idea. I think it's the only time I've seen that man cry."

Tears welled in Savannah's eyes at that thought. "I'm so, so happy for you two. This could not be more perfect." She stared at her in awe. "No wonder you didn't want a beer."

Liz giggled. "Well, yeah. Can't drink for nine months. Not with a little Maxwell growing inside me."

"I can't. It's too amazing."

"Oh, and that party I mentioned for next weekend. It's a baby announcement. So, don't tell anyone else."

She mimicked zipping her lips closed. "These lips are sealed. Though I'm glad I only have to wait a week because I'd die, keeping this from everyone longer than that."

"I've been dying just these last couple of weeks."

"Did you know at my graduation?"

Liz nodded. "But we weren't sure if we should tell anyone yet."

Savannah threw her arms around Liz again and squealed with joy. As they were both jumping up and down and celebrating the new little Maxwell, an uproar exploded from the rest of the room.

Savannah startled away from Liz, and they both

had surprised looks on their faces. Then, they turned to the row of TVs as one.

And on-screen was none other than Lucas Atwood.

Savannah's mouth dropped open. "Is today the draft?"

"Sure looks like it."

"Where was he drafted?" she asked.

Then, the announcer answered her question and the reason for the loud cheers from the crowd. "Vanderbilt star Lucas Atwood drafted to the Washington Wizards!"

"He's coming to DC," Liz said in shock.

"You have got to be fucking kidding me."

8

Meet the Fam

"Now, don't be nervous," Savannah said to Dylan.

"I'm not nervous." Dylan rolled her eyes and stepped out of the backseat of the car.

"Meeting my family is kind of…a lot."

"You're scaring her off," Easton said. "Your family is fine."

"You almost fainted the first time you met them."

"I did not. And anyway, I didn't *know* you were a Maxwell when we started dating. You just sprang that on me by having me meet your father."

"Do you know how many senators I've met in this town?" Dylan asked. "It's no sweat."

Savannah nodded as she shut her door and headed toward Brady's place. She was only saying this stuff to Dylan because she was nervous about bringing someone to his place. She'd always been like that. And she'd only known Dylan such a short time. They'd gotten drinks earlier this week after work and then again for her to meet Easton. They'd all hit it off, and she felt like she was finally finding her rhythm in the city.

Easton knocked on the door twice before entering. Brady and Liz were standing in the entranceway. He looked ever the dapper congressman in a suit with his arm around his loving wife. Liz was dressed to kill in a blue number that revealed what she had so wanted to hide these last couple of weeks. It honestly wasn't even fair how beautiful they were together. So fucking lucky to have found that.

Brady shook Easton's hand and then smiled broadly when he saw his sister.

"Savi," Brady said, pulling her in for a hug. "How are you settling in?"

"I like it so far. Work is…work."

"So I've been told." He glanced to Liz. "I hear your boss is a jerk."

Savannah narrowed her eyes at Liz. "Snitch."

Liz shrugged one shoulder. "You can't expect me to keep things from my husband."

"I didn't tell Easton about you!"

Liz shrugged with a grin.

Brady laughed. "It's not like I'm going to stomp down to the newspaper and tell them to treat my sister better. You'll find your feet. They're just doing their job."

"That's what I keep saying," Dylan said.

Brady's eyes swept to Dylan, who froze in place. Savannah would have laughed if she hadn't seen that same expression on hundreds of other women. She hadn't met anyone immune to her brother's charms. No matter how many senators you'd met, there was only one Brady Maxwell.

"And who is this?" he asked with that debonair smile.

Liz just shook her head. "You're worse than your brother."

He shot her a look. "How insulting."

"This is Dylan," Savannah said. "She works with me at the paper."

"Hi," Dylan said. She'd lost some of her bravado in the wake of Brady's inimitable presence.

"Nice to meet you." He held his hand out, and she shook gratefully. "Any friend of Savi's is a friend of mine."

"That is how you met your wife," Savannah muttered under her breath.

"Oh my God, you two," Liz said. "Let the girl breathe. Thank you so much for coming, Dylan. Feel free to help yourself to food and drinks."

"You look lovely," Dylan finally said. "How far along are you?"

Liz laughed. "Can you already tell?"

Dylan shrugged. "My family is Dominican, and I have four older sisters. I know the look. You glow."

"Why, thank you. That's good to hear." Liz protectively put her hand on her stomach.

"Liz, you're pregnant?" Easton asked with a huge smile on his face. "That's great. Congratulations."

"See I keep my secrets," Savannah muttered.

She laughed softly. "Cat's out of the bag. Come inside. We're about to tell the others."

Savannah followed Liz and Brady into the living room and found it full of her family. Her mother and father were standing with another senator from their home state as well as his wife and kids. She found Clay teasing his wife, Andrea, in the corner. She looked like she might stab him or kiss him. It was hard to tell with those two. The Atwoods were here with their daughter, Alice, who just looked annoyed. Oh, teenage angst.

Following that line of vision, she found their eldest son and Lucas's older brother, Chris, talking to Clay's law partner, Gigi.

For a while, Savannah had had the biggest crush on Chris. It was a dumb childhood thing. He was ten years older than her, and it had ended when she realized what she wanted was right in front of her.

And there *he* was.

She held her breath at the sight of Lucas. She hadn't known whether or not he would show up. Whether or not he was even in the city yet. If the team had sent him here for training or if he had to be somewhere else at a camp. If he was living it up in

Nashville with his fancy new bonus check. She didn't know because she hadn't spoken to him. She hadn't congratulated him or apologized or anything. And he hadn't reached out to her either.

Her stomach clenched when his eyes found her in the room and then hastily darted away. As if those hateful words they'd screamed at each other were their new reality. Maybe they were.

"Thank you all for coming," Brady said once everyone was assembled. "It's a pleasure, having you all in my home tonight. We just have one announcement before the party continues."

He looked at Liz with adoration in his eyes. It said everything Savannah had always known about them. They were perfect together.

Liz turned back to the crowd, put her hand on her stomach, and said, "I'm pregnant."

A gasp went up through the crowd and then a ring of congratulations as everyone rushed forward, eager to give their well wishes to the happy couple. Savannah tugged Dylan around the crowd to the buffet table and reached out for some finger food.

"I'm starving. I hardly ate before this," Savannah told her.

Dylan shook her head. "Your brother is so much hotter than his picture."

"Uh...ew," Savannah said as she nibbled on a sandwich and added carrots, dip, and a cookie to her plate.

"I was a total idiot." She fluffed her curly hair and sighed. "I mean...have I ever been speechless in my life?"

"I really don't think so."

"Do you have another one of those lying around? I could be into joining the family."

Savannah laughed and shook her head. "Nope. All out of Maxwell men."

"Damn! What about that guy? Is he taken?"

Savannah knew who Dylan was talking about before she turned around. Because, of course, even though the room was full of people, including many other young men who worked with Brady, it was Lucas Atwood who had drawn Dylan's eye.

"That...is Lucas."

Dylan arched one of her perfectly maintained eyebrows. "By that response, I guess he's taken?"

"No. Actually, he's not. He's very much single."

"Excellent. Introduce me?"

Savannah opened her mouth to tell her friend there was no chance in hell, but how exactly could she even explain that? She'd only known Dylan for a couple of weeks. The nonsense with Lucas had been going on for years.

"Yeah, sure," she finally said. She tossed her finished plate of food and grabbed a drink for the nerves.

After taking a large gulp, she navigated the room until she was standing before Lucas. He arched an eyebrow at her. She could practically read what he was thinking. *What the hell are you doing over here? Don't you have someone else to bother? Like your boyfriend?*

Savannah pushed her shoulders back. "Lucas, this is my friend Dylan. Dylan, this is Lucas."

"Hey." Dylan thrust her hand out, and Lucas shook it.

"Nice to meet you," Lucas said. His eyes flickered to Savannah's and then back to Dylan where he gave her the most charming look. "How do you know Savi exactly?"

"We work at the *Post* together. I saved her butt her first day on the job, and she's torturing me by insisting I come to family parties with her." Dylan smiled coquettishly and leaned toward Lucas. "What about you? Is she also torturing you?"

Savannah nearly spat out her drink. *Good job, Dylan. Straight As for awkwardness.*

"Savi and I grew up together. Our parents are best friends," Lucas added smoothly. "She has a way of torturing everyone around her, doesn't she?"

Dylan nudged Savannah. "In the best way."

"Mmm…"

"And what about you?" Lucas asked, shifting ever so slightly so that his attention was focused intently on Dylan. A purposeful move that made Savannah's stomach clench. "Tell me about yourself."

Dylan grinned. "I'm from DC, but my parents are Dominican. I graduated from…"

Savannah only listened with half an ear as Dylan went on about herself. What Savannah was more focused on was the body language. The way Dylan leaned into him, playfully swatted him, laughed whenever he opened his mouth. Savannah had promised Dylan the party wouldn't be boring, but she hadn't expected this.

How could she have though? She hadn't thought Lucas would even *be* at this party. And she'd known that Dylan was looking—part of the draw was all of Brady's cute employees—but not…Lucas.

Either she needed to leave them alone and walk away from this or she needed to end it. Because she couldn't stand here any longer.

"Hey," Savannah said, drawing Lucas's attention back to her. "Can we talk?"

"We're talking now."

"Alone," she said pointedly.

Lucas looked like he was going to say no and tell her to fuck off, but then he nodded once.

Savannah shot Dylan what she hoped was a reassuring smile. "Sorry to steal him. It'll just be a minute."

Dylan shrugged. "I'm kind of starving anyway. Don't abandon me too long. I don't know anyone!"

"As if it's hard for you to make friends," Savannah teased.

Dylan grinned slyly. "True."

Dylan meandered back to the table lined with

food, and Savannah nodded her head into the other room. Her eyes flit self-consciously to where Easton was standing with his colleagues. He laughed and joked and seemed to be the center of that tiny universe. His attention was so diverted that she was sure he didn't even see her slip out.

Savannah pulled open the door to the guest bedroom. "Get in."

"What do you want, Savannah?"

"I want to talk to you."

He grasped her arm. "Last time we spoke, you said you hated me and then literally left the city to escape me. Why should I go in there?"

"Do you want to have this conversation where everyone can hear us?"

"What do *I* have to hide?" he asked mercilessly.

"Lucas," she growled low.

He sighed and stepped into the bedroom. She carefully closed the door behind them and leaned back on it. This was stupid. She knew it was. Everything that had to do with Lucas was stupid. But she'd hated standing there and watching him flirt with her friend. Of course, it was hypocritical of her, considering she had a boyfriend, but she couldn't change how she felt. Especially not when they were still on rocky terms.

"I can't believe you were just flirting with her." She ground her teeth together. Why was that the first thing that had come out of her mouth? Why couldn't she have just said what she actually wanted to say instead of letting the anger get to her?

"Is there something wrong with me flirting with her?"

"You did it on purpose," she accused. "You're unbelievable."

He laughed and walked away from her. "This is why I'm here? Fuck, Savi. Is it wrong for me to want you to feel an ounce of what I feel when you walk in here with him?"

"Seriously? That's what this is about?"

"I can't with you. Move out of the way. I don't need to stand here and hear more of your bullshit. You made yourself perfectly clear in Nashville." He strode forward until he was nearly in her face.

"Ugh! I don't even know why I bother with you!" She pushed him away. "I was going to apologize, you know!"

"Apologize?" He snorted. "Yeah. As if you're even capable."

"Why do you make me so crazy?"

"I have no idea. But you're batshit!"

She glared at him and crossed her arms. "But why her?"

"You brought her over to me," he spat. "And anyway, you've been dating Easton for three goddamn years. Do you really think you have room to talk?"

The words hit her in the face. She was being irrational. Utterly irrational. This wasn't even why she had come back here. Yes, she didn't like him flirting with Dylan in front of her, but that hardly mattered. Fuck, why was it so impossible to think around him?

"You're right," Savannah said softly.

"Excuse me?"

"You're right, okay?"

"I am?" He sounded skeptical.

"I don't have room to talk. Easton and I are together. So, you can flirt with whoever you want. That wasn't even why I asked you back here."

"Why did you?"

"Well, first, I wanted to congratulate you. You actually did it. You're an NBA star."

He chuckled softly. "Not exactly. But thanks."

"You'll prove yourself. And it's so awesome that you're living your dream."

"What about your dream? Did you go to your audition?"

She chewed on her lip. She'd been debating about going to the *Seven Brides for Seven Brothers* audition. She had everything prepared. But it didn't make it any easier. She was rusty. She'd been out of it too long.

"That's a hobby," she corrected. "And, yeah…I think I'm going to go."

"You'll let me know how it goes?"

She shrugged. "If you want me to."

"I do."

"When do you start with basketball?"

"Next week. I'll be swamped all summer, preparing for the season."

"You'll like that. You've always liked being busy. Are you happy to be in DC?" she asked.

"It'll be nice, being near my family again. And your family. Are you happy I'm in DC?"

"That's complicated. But I'm glad that you got everything you wanted."

He snorted. "Not everything."

She pushed her hair behind her ear to avoid the implication in those words. "And I guess, secondly, I wanted to say that I'm…sorry about what happened in Nashville."

She looked up at him under thick black lashes and felt for a second as if she were exposing her soul to him. He seemed to see her like no one else. Their years as friends growing up together had just changed their dynamic.

"I got drunk and acted like an idiot," she continued. "I put myself in a bad position and then took out my anger on you. You were the gentleman who stopped me from doing anything stupid."

"Uh…"

She tilted her head. "Well, from doing anything stupider than getting wasted and dancing on tables. You stopped us from happening again."

"Not exactly, Sav."

"What do you mean, not exactly? You said that… you stopped us."

"I did," he confirmed. "After we kissed."

"Kissed?"

"Yeah, Savi, we kissed."

His words opened something in her. Then, it all came back. A rush of memories that she had clearly repressed.

They'd kissed. Oh God, they'd kissed that night. Savagely, wantonly. His hands in her hair, on her waist, her breasts. The need between them. Fuck, fuck, fuck.

She suddenly felt like she might throw up.

9

Don't Throw It Away

"I can't believe we…" she muttered.

Lucas stepped closer. So close. Dangerously close. The small distance that made her brain go fuzzy. That made her remember things she shouldn't and want things she couldn't have.

"You honestly don't remember?" he asked with raised eyebrows.

"You said nothing happened."

She was desperate for it to be true. For these new memories to be false.

"Yeah, because I thought we were playing that game. Jesus, we kissed, and you begged me for more. You wanted me inside you, but I walked."

Savannah leaned forward and buried her face in her hands. "Oh God. Oh God. Oh God."

She couldn't believe this. She had blocked that night out. She'd blacked out. So much of it was foggy.

Only bits and pieces of it had come back to her. But she had a distinct memory of asking him if he was scared. She hadn't known what it meant. But now that the pieces were all back together, it hit her like a two-by-four.

She'd kissed Lucas.

She was dating Easton, and she'd kissed Lucas. It was bad enough, what they'd done together in the past. That they'd…slept together on the Fourth of July all those years ago. But they moved on from that. It didn't happen again. It was so long ago. She'd thought that she wouldn't give in again. And now, here she was, with the knowledge that she'd fucked up.

"I have to tell him," she whispered. She tried to hold in the inner panic that was taking over her body.

"Savi…"

"I have to be honest. He's going to hate me."

"Look, you were trashed, and clearly…it meant nothing to you," Lucas said. "You didn't even remember."

"That doesn't mean it didn't happen," she whisper-shouted at him. Her eyes found his, and she stared hazily. Her body began to tremble. "It happened. And I said it would never happen again. He hates you for a reason."

"I know."

"So…I have to go tell him."

She straightened and reached for the door handle with a shaking hand, but Lucas was there.

He pushed the door closed. "You can't go barging in there, looking like this and acting all crazy. Even if you're going to tell him, you shouldn't do it like this."

"I have to," she said, her throat sore and tears threatening to fall.

"Think for a second. Do you want to kiss me? Is this what you want? Because if it's not, then what are you throwing away all of this for?"

She stared up at him in surprise. "Are you defending Easton?"

"I'm defending your happiness," he said. "Do I want you with him? Hell fucking no. But I don't want to be the reason your light goes out."

"What am I going to do?" she whispered in agony.

"Nothing." He sighed. "You don't want this. We've had every opportunity, and it's not what you want. So, just let it go. We shouldn't have to keep hurting each other."

"Even if this means the end?" she couldn't help but ask.

He looked away as if the very idea was too hard to consider. "I always thought that you were going to be mine. I knew from an early age that I would never love anyone the way that I loved you." His eyes met her. "But I can't control if you don't feel the same way."

"Lucas…" she gasped, tears finally coming to her eyes.

"I'd fight for you to the ends of the earth if you gave me a spark of hope. But I'm not going to keep fighting a losing battle. I won't say I'm happy for you. I'll just…disappear." He leaned forward and swiped the tears from her cheeks. "Don't cry for me. You just got everything you wanted."

He pulled the door open, gently pushing her away from where she had been standing. Then, he disappeared through it without another glance. Her heart was trying to wrest its way out of her chest. She felt like she might collapse. If she'd thought their argument in Nashville was bad, this was so much worse.

He'd just…left.

He'd wanted to protect her happiness over her having to tell Easton what had happened between them. He was actually…bowing out of the fight.

It seemed impossible that one short conversation could end up here.

How could she even return to the party? What would she say to everyone? What would she say to Easton?

He deserved to know.

She knew that.

She should have never done it. But it didn't excuse what she had done. It didn't make it okay. Even if she wasn't going to be with Lucas, Easton deserved better.

She wiped the last tear that had fallen down her

cheek and tried to rally. She had to get through the rest of this party and then figure out where to go from here. Because Lucas was right about one thing at least. She couldn't just fly out there right now and blurt it all out. Her entire family was here. Half of Brady's employees were here. Everyone she knew and loved. She'd have to find a better time.

Straightening out her clothes and hoping that she didn't look like she'd been crying, she exited the guest bedroom. Thankfully, the hallway was empty, and she carefully slipped back into the party.

Dylan was standing with one of Brady's employees, smiling and carrying on like Savannah hadn't abandoned her. Liz was chatting with Victoria. Easton's eyes caught her across the distance, and he tilted his chin to indicate she should come over. She nodded and headed in his direction, looking around the full room.

Lucas was nowhere to be seen.

Maybe he'd really left after all.

"Hey baby," Easton said, pulling her close and kissing her cheek.

She held in her flinch. Her mind still closely focused on the horrible thing she had done and had to tell him about. But she couldn't show it. Not yet.

"Hey. How's the party going?" she asked.

"Good so far. I'm surprised at how many people showed up. Even Jake showed. And you know how much of a flake he is."

"Right. Jake."

"Dylan seems to be into Curtis."

"She's good with people."

"I saw her talking with Lucas too," he added casually.

"Yeah. I introduced them," she said, monotone.

Easton arched an eyebrow in surprise. "How's he doing?"

"I don't know," she lied. "What does it matter?"

He clearly liked that response because his smile brightened to the megawatt that had made her fall for him. The perfect hair and jaw and smile and eyes and everything. The tennis body she'd died for that first day. The chemistry that had ignited at first touch. The everything that looked like it was crumbling into pieces all around her.

"Are you okay?" he asked when he noticed her expression.

"I'm just beat, I think. Work has been so rough. It's hard to decompress."

"I know." He slipped an arm around her shoulders. "We don't have to stay long."

"That'd be great," she said with a half-smile.

He kissed her hair and went back to talking to his colleagues. Dylan returned to their circle soon enough. Having her there ended up being a great distraction because hardly anyone noticed how quiet Savannah was. And only she noticed when Lucas slipped back into the room to talk to his brother.

For a split second, both Lucas's and Chris's attention were focused on her, and then they both darted away.

Oh God, did Chris know?

Her stomach twisted at that thought. Because if Chris knew…would it get back to Brady? She didn't want it to spiral out of control.

She tried not to let her mind corkscrew into a dangerous paranoia. There was nothing she could do about anything tonight. She'd have to figure it all out later and be more present now.

"Do you need another drink?" Easton asked.

"Oh, no. I'm not really drinking tonight," she told him. Because drinking was definitely a crux of one of her problems.

"Huh. Okay. Just me then."

He stepped back and faced the entire room and raised his glass high.

"Excuse me. Excuse me. Can I have everyone's attention?"

Savannah looked at him in confusion. What was he doing? A toast?

The room quieted almost instantly, and everyone's attention was rapt on Easton standing at the front of the room.

"I'd like to take this opportunity to thank Brady and Liz for hosting this amazing party tonight. I'm so thankful for them, and I can't wait to meet their new addition to the household."

Cheers went up around the room as everyone agreed with Easton.

Brady raised a glass to Easton and winked. Liz just hugged her belly and smiled. The genuine happiness that radiated from them was almost sickening.

"And while I have your attention, I want to turn to the love of my life and ask a question."

Savannah's eyes widened as Easton turned to face her. He withdrew a blue box from his coat pocket and dropped to one knee. He opened the box to reveal an enormous haloed diamond.

Her stomach dropped out of her body, and her heart screeched to a halt. Her hands flew to her mouth.

Easton looked up at her with earnest, kind eyes. "Savannah, will you marry me?"

A...proposal.

He was...proposing.

Oh, fucking hell.

What...what was she supposed to do? She'd been planning to tell him that she'd kissed Lucas...and he was asking her to marry him? In front of everyone that she knew. Her parents and siblings and their wives and all their friends and...Lucas.

Everyone.

Tears came to her eyes again, unbidden.

She'd dreamed of this moment. Hoped for this moment. Envisioned exactly how it would all go.

And now that it was here, it was both magical… and horrifying.

Because she wanted to say yes. But she shouldn't say yes. And she couldn't say no.

"Yes," she choked out.

Easton plucked the ring out of the box and slid it onto her finger. Then, he scooped her up into his arms and swung her around in a circle. She could dimly hear the cheers through the fog that was her brain. And her eyes snagged for just a moment, just a brief second, on Lucas's retreating back.

10

Truth

The rest of the party was painful.

Painful to keep a smile on her face.

To fake the happiness that she should have felt.

To ignore the look of concern that kept flashing on Liz's face.

It was a relief when Easton finally decided to bow out. His colleagues kept congratulating him. Offering him drink after drink, which he took with a careful smile and quick laugh as if this were his moment.

Dylan oohed and aahed over the ring. She wanted to celebrate next week after work when she had more free time. And promised that she'd be planning a girls' night soon for it. Maybe this would thaw the frost from Savannah's other colleagues at the newspaper.

Since Savannah was the only one still sober, she dropped Dylan off at her apartment and then drove Easton home to their place in Georgetown. She had to circle the block a half-dozen times before she finally slid into an open spot.

Easton slung an arm over her shoulders as they navigated the short distance to their building. He was nuzzling her neck and whispering sweet, drunken nothings into her ear. She laughed as he nipped at her earlobe and swatted him away.

"We should get you another drink," he said.

"Let's open up a bottle when we get inside."

She led them up the stairs and turned the key in the lock. Their home didn't quite feel warm and welcoming. Their separate belongings trying to merge into one but not yet managing it. Her style was too rigid—stiff throw pillows, black-and-white portraits, crisp furniture. His showed signs that he'd been a bachelor for many years with hand-me-down belongings that he'd made his own. For a second, that felt like their relationship.

Three years together in Chapel Hill, and they'd never moved in together. She liked her space. He'd had roommates. They'd stayed at her place more than his because it was quiet, and there was no one to interrupt them. And she could see the stark differences tonight.

Her own melancholy and euphoria bleeding together into something like disaster.

Easton strolled lazily into the kitchen and pulled out a bottle of bourbon from the top shelf. He poured a knuckle's worth into two glasses and then brought one over to her. She took it to cover her shaking hands. He held his aloft.

"To us."

She raised the glass, clinking it against his, but didn't say anything. Just downed the dark liquid in a big, long gulp. It burned like fire down her throat. She held back her cough and shook her head once to clear it.

Easton took the glass from her hand and dropped it onto the coffee table. He pulled her into his arms. Not the drunken embrace she had imagined but a dance. He gently cupped her waist before bringing their palms together. His eyes were intense and full of love. So much love as he swayed them back and forth on their hardwood floor. The creak of the wood the only music.

She rested her head against his chest, leaning into his familiar warmth. It was normal, natural even. They had always been good together. When she closed her eyes, it was enough that she could smell the faint touch of bourbon on his breath and the musky smell underneath that belonged solely to Easton.

Let her mind drift back to the days when they'd first gotten together and he had no idea who she was. That she was a Maxwell with a political dynasty for a family. And a name that opened doors and made laws and ruled in its own way.

When she'd thought he was just a UNC student who taught tennis on the side. Just a sexy man with ripped six-pack abs that could make her forget entirely about the boy who'd left for Nashville. When she hadn't known that he wanted to be a politician. That he would work for her brother as he worked his way up the ladder. Or that they'd move here together to follow their dreams.

She'd thought that she was rebelling by picking the hot tennis instructor. Instead, he had fallen perfectly in line with her family's expectations of her. Proving that the tattooed motorcyclist was just a phase. And the dumb frat boys they didn't know about were nothing at all.

But she had fallen for him so completely. So easily. She'd overlooked it. What was one fault—which no one else would consider a fault—in the profile of a perfect man? The kind of man who could forgive her for cheating and give her a second chance when she didn't deserve one. When she still had to be around the other man, when he did. And who, despite all of that, wanted to marry her.

She glanced at the ring on her left ring finger over his shoulder. It was enormous. She had no idea how he'd afforded it. If he'd gotten money from her father to help with it. It wouldn't surprise her. Only the best for his little girl.

"Where are you at tonight, Savi?" Easton whispered into her ear.

"I'm here with you."

"You seem so far away."

103

He pulled back and twirled her in place. Then, he dragged her back against him. His signature grin was plastered on his face.

"Is it still just work?" he asked.

She opened her mouth to say something and then shook her head.

He stroked the line of her hair, playing with the dark brown strands. His knuckles dragged against her jawline, and then his thumb played across her bottom lip.

"Talk to me. Did I overwhelm you?" he asked with a huff of a laugh. "Should I have taken you to a fancy dinner instead? When I talked to Brady, he suggested the party. I agreed with him."

"Brady knew?" she muttered.

"Well, I asked him when we were gone last weekend in Chapel Hill. I'd already spoken with your father."

She nodded slightly, shocked by the old-fashioned gesture. "I didn't know."

"It wouldn't have been much of a surprise if they'd told you." He drew her in for a soft kiss. "Is it the ring?" He brought the giant thing between them to look at. "Did you want something simpler? Just one enormous rock instead of a halo of them? You'd never said what kind of diamonds you liked."

She hadn't, had she?

"No. This is perfect," she said. It wasn't what she would have picked, but it was beautiful.

"Then, what is it?"

He was so earnest. She wanted to save him from this. She'd thought she could hold out until tomorrow. Put some distance between the engagement and what she was about to say.

Lucas had said that it didn't matter. She didn't need to tell Easton because it was never going to happen again. That it would ruin everything. And she suspected Lucas was right. That if she didn't tell Easton what had happened, all would be well. They'd get married, have the requisite two and a half children, and move to the suburbs. He'd go into politics while she quit the paper to stay home with the kids and support his career. She could see it so clearly, as if it were a movie reel.

Harbor this secret until it festered and turned rotten inside of her. Until she resented him for his earlier forgiveness and hated herself for keeping this from him. Despised herself for becoming a Stepford wife because of her guilt.

The lie hung on the tip of her tongue.

Forget it.

Nothing had happened.

She was happy.

Instead, she met his clear gaze, swallowed back bile, and said, "Lucas and I kissed."

Easton went preternaturally still. A kind of stillness that came from utter shock and horror and vengeance. There were no words. There was just silence and twin flames in his beautiful eyes.

"Say something," she whispered.

He took a step back. His hands dropped to his sides. He looked at her as if he didn't recognize her. As if she were a ghost in their apartment, not fully corporeal. Something that he could pass through to get to reality again.

"Easton," she murmured.

"What would you have me say?" he asked, his voice low and gravelly.

"Anything."

He huffed a harsh laugh, cold and full of razor-sharp edges. "You don't want to hear me say anything."

"I do though."

She wanted his anger. She deserved it. Had been anticipating it. His silence was worse, she realized. So much worse.

"When?" was the word he finally bit out.

"At his graduation. I...blacked out and didn't remember. He said nothing happened, and then tonight, he told me that we kissed."

Easton narrowed his eyes. She could see his sharp mind piecing it all together. "*Of course* he did."

"I'm sorry," she said softly. "I'm so, so sorry."

He shook his head, turning away from the words. He stumbled backward and reached for the keys that she'd left in a dish by the front door.

"What are you doing?" she asked, suddenly frantic.

"Going out."

"You're drunk. You can't drive."

"Fine. I'll take a cab." He threw the keys in the direction of the dish and wrenched the door open. "Don't fucking follow me."

Then, he was through the door and vaulting down the stairs to the main floor. She heard the ground-level door open, and then he was gone.

To where? She had no idea.

Out. Gone. Away.

Away from her.

And what she'd told him.

The truth she had confessed that would break him.

Savannah sank onto the sofa and stared at the door, willing him to come back, to talk to her, to figure this out.

But the door remained closed.

And he didn't come back.

11

Runaway

"I haven't heard from him. But if Brady or I do hear anything, we'll call you right away," Liz said over the phone. "You could always come over here if you want."

"No, I want to be here in case he shows up," Savannah told her.

She hadn't slept all night. Dark circles ringed her eyes, but they weren't swollen or puffy or red. She hadn't cried. Not one tear. She was too numb and horrified and worried.

Really worried.

Easton had left almost exactly twelve hours ago, and he was still nowhere to be seen. He wasn't answering texts or calls. He hadn't been online in all that time. No one else had heard from him. And she had no idea where he was, if he was okay, or if he was lying in a gutter somewhere.

"All right," Liz said. "Should I come over there to be with you?"

Savannah held her aching stomach. She hadn't been able to eat anything. Just stared around in stress and misery.

"I don't know."

"Okay, executive decision: I am coming over there. You have been alone too long. I'll see you in a half hour."

Savannah couldn't argue. She probably had been alone too long. She'd been left to think about all the ways she could have told Easton what had happened with Lucas that wouldn't have resulted in him running off in the middle of the night while he was intoxicated. Pretty much every other scenario.

She hung up the phone and set it faceup on the coffee table. She double-checked the volume was on for the hundredth time. Then, she stared up at the ceiling in dismay. She didn't know what else to do. If she went out looking for him, then he might just show up while she was gone. His friends claimed that they hadn't seen him. They hadn't been living there long enough for her to know where he'd go.

She was straight-up fucked.

She had expected anger. She had expected him to scream at her and rage. To say that he *knew* it. That he'd been right.

Not this.

Never this.

Easton wasn't someone who ran away from his problems. He was a problem solver. His mother was a therapist, for Christ's sake. He'd grown up, knowing how to manage stress and deal with other people's problems. In fact, he'd always been a little too understanding of her own issues. So running wasn't even something she had considered.

The silence loomed darker. Every added hour stretched thicker and more tangible. Diving into space and only finding a yawning vacuum prepared to suck her into oblivion.

Sometime in the emptiness, someone knocked on the door. Liz must have shown up. Savannah hadn't been tracking time, except to say another hour had passed since Easton disappeared.

She hoisted her numb body off of the couch and opened the door. She gasped at the sight of him standing at the entrance to their apartment.

"Easton," she whispered.

Her heartbeat roared in her ears. Her hands trembled. Life swooshed back into her. His presence here replacing the worry of what-if. But the hard set of his jaw did nothing to dispel her other fears.

"Can I come in?" he asked.

"Of course. You live here." She stepped back, gesturing him into his own apartment. Her world felt like it was standing on a precarious axis, waiting to tip over.

He stepped inside, and she closed the door behind

him. She memorized his features in that moment. Noticed the five o'clock shadow growing in along his jawline. The mussed hair and rumpled state of his clothing. But his eyes were clear, assessing, weighing.

"Where were you?" she gasped out. She couldn't help it. She'd been so worried.

"At first, I thought I would go find Lucas," he said slowly, calmly. "Probably couldn't beat the shit out of him, but thought it would be worth a try."

Savannah said nothing. She didn't think he wanted her to speak.

"Couldn't find him. I don't know where he's staying in the city. And the more I searched, the more I realized that I wanted answers from him."

From him and not her.

"I wanted to know why he'd told you about the supposed kiss now. Why he'd thought it was a good idea to remind you that you had blacked out. If it had even happened. How much of it did he make up to get between us?"

Savannah put her hand to her lips. Oh God.

"It was drunken ramblings and anger that brought me to a bar where I tried to drink myself through the entire liquor shelf." He tilted his head to the side and turned to face her fully. "That was when I realized that there must have been a reason you believed him. I wanted to blame Lucas. It's easy to blame Lucas. But you thought it was true when he told you."

She swallowed. She had immediately known it for

truth. Her heart hadn't wanted to believe that anything had happened with Lucas, so she had believed him when he said it hadn't. As soon as he'd admitted that they'd kissed, it had all rushed back.

"So, what I want to know is, what else have you been keeping from me?" His voice was quiet and chilled. A killing calm in his demeanor that put her on edge.

"Nothing," she said at once. "I didn't even keep that from you. I didn't...I wouldn't. I had to tell you."

"Savannah," he said calmly. "Just tell me the truth."

"I am."

"Tell me." His voice rose slightly.

Her pulse quickened. The kiss had been the worst of it. But it hadn't been all of it, had it?

"I stayed at Lucas's place that night in Nashville."

He nodded. "And?"

"My mother orchestrated it. I was in the spare bedroom. I didn't think it would matter. It was just one night."

"And then you went out with him and got wasted."

"Yes. And we...danced," she confessed. "At the party. But that was it. I just hung out with his friends. We acted stupid. Normal college shit."

"Except that you went home with him that night, and then you two kissed. If that was all that happened," he said with a disbelief that said he doubted it'd stopped there.

"We just kissed."

"But how would you know?" he asked. "You were blackout drunk. You said so yourself. How do you know he didn't fuck you that night, Savannah?"

"Lucas wouldn't."

Easton laughed, cutting off what she would have said next. "Sure he wouldn't."

"We didn't!" she insisted.

"Have there been other times? Other times you had been alone and maybe forgot what had happened?"

"No," she gasped at his accusatory tone.

Yes, she had done something wrong and owned up to it, but that didn't mean they had slept together. Or that they'd slept together before this. Easton knew about the one time she had been with Lucas, and she'd been so careful around him up until his graduation.

"Nothing else? Not even a little bit? This is your chance, Savannah."

She stared at him, racking her brain, trying to think of anything that would damn her. But she didn't know. They hadn't done anything. Not for a long time. Not since…wait.

"We saw each other when I was gone for Liz's bachelorette party at Hilton Head."

"Old habits do die hard."

"No, it wasn't like that. I was on the beach already. He was drunk and high and found me and, like, confessed his undying love for me. I told him to leave me alone, and the guys dragged him away. Everyone was there for it. Liz will tell you."

"I believe you," he said with a nod. "But why didn't you tell me when it happened?"

She had wanted to. She thought about it when she first got back. But then the old fears came back. The fears that said Lucas would cause trouble, and her relationship with Easton was so good, so solid. No need to rock the boat.

She shook her head. She had no response.

"Why didn't you tell me that you were auditioning for a play?"

"How did you…" She trailed off.

"How did I know? Really? That's the question?"

"No," she said quickly. "I just…have you been reading my emails?"

He looked at her, aghast. "Of course not. It came in the freaking mail, Savannah."

"Oh," she muttered. She'd forgotten about that. She'd gotten the email first and tossed the papers as soon as it came in.

"I had to look it up to even see what it was. I didn't know that you were interested in theater. I kept waiting for the day that you would tell me that you had filled it out and sent it in. That you had been given an audition date. That something you clearly loved was moving into place, and you never did tell me. Why is that?"

She didn't answer because she didn't have an answer. But he did.

"Because you hide your true self," he said. He took another step back from her. "You hide who you are. Maybe you don't even know who you really are. And the further you slipped away, the tighter I held on. But it didn't matter. Still doesn't matter."

He strode away from her, determined and lethally calm. He'd already thought this all through. Everything she had said just confirmed his own assumptions.

"This isn't about Lucas," he went on. "This is about your lies and secrets. The ones you keep from me and, worse, the ones you keep from yourself. I don't want to be with that person."

Her heart stopped. Those words. That blow.

"Easton," she whispered.

"I've put up with it long enough. I let you walk all over me. Let you have your way. But I'm done." His eyes flicked to hers.

"You're done?" she whispered unable to comprehend what he was saying.

"I think we just need space to figure this out. Be apart until you can figure out who you are and what you want. Because, right now, I don't think you can commit fully to a relationship. And if this just throws you into Lucas's arms, then I guess I proved my point.

Why work on yourself when you can have something convenient, right?"

She winced at the harsh words.

"I don't want Lucas," she told him.

"Yeah. We'll see." He grabbed his laptop bag and threw it over his shoulder. "I'm just going to pack a suitcase. Gary said I could crash at his place for a while."

"You can stay here," she whispered. "I can stay with Liz."

"Not sure it'd be in my best interest to be surrounded by your stuff. So, just take the apartment. It was what you wanted anyway."

He disappeared into the bedroom and came out less than five minutes later with a suitcase. It looked so official with his bag. Shock started to set in. Full-on shock. Easton was *leaving her*. She had never once thought this would ever happen.

She slipped the diamond ring from her finger. "Here."

He stared down at it, and for the first time, his resolve cracked. The loving, kind, caring man she'd fallen for shone through. He looked like he was going to take it all back. Decide that he couldn't live without her and help her fix her issues. But then he just pocketed the ring, roughly kissed her cheek, and pulled the door open.

Liz stood, silhouetted in the doorframe. Her eyes

were wide as she took in the scene before her—the suitcase, rumpled man, and shell-shocked woman.

"Hi, Easton," she said softly, carefully.

"Liz," he said with a nod. "If you'll excuse me."

"Going somewhere?"

"She'll fill you in."

"I'm sure she will," Liz said with an arched eyebrow. "I'm going to guess you're canceling my tennis lesson."

He ground his teeth. "I think we'll take a summer hiatus."

"Is that what you're calling what you're doing?"

"Don't," he barked.

Liz took a step back. "You seem to have made up your mind all on your own."

Easton nodded curtly and then bustled out the door without a backward glance. Liz turned her attention back to Savannah.

"You'll stay with me," she insisted before stepping a foot inside. "We'll figure it out."

Savannah nodded. She still didn't have words.

"Oh, come here." Liz staggered forward into the room and wrapped her arms around Savannah.

Liz didn't tell Savannah it would be all right. That everything would work out. She didn't bait her with platitudes. Liz knew firsthand what it was like to suffer for love. Knew all the things that could go wrong in a relationship. They'd come out on top, but nothing had made it easy as she went through it. And Savannah knew Liz wouldn't lie to her.

So, she packed her own suitcase and followed Liz out of her apartment. Wondered what the hell she was going to do. And if she had just made the worst mistake of her entire life.

12

One Less Ring

"You can stay in the guest room," Liz said.

She drew Savannah into the house that she'd fled only yesterday with a diamond ring on her finger. Now, she was entering it all alone.

"Thanks," she whispered.

Brady appeared from out of the bedroom. He was dressed down in a T-shirt and shorts. It was weird, even for Savannah, to see him like that. He was a suit through and through.

"What's going on?" he asked, confusion written on his face.

"Easton left Savannah," Liz said.

"What?" Brady asked, his voice low and deadly. "He just proposed yesterday."

"Yeah, I'll fill you in," Liz said. "Suffice it to say, Savi wasn't really ready for that move yet."

"Do I need to go find him? I can probably

threaten him within an inch of his life for hurting you."

"No," Savannah said with a shake of her head. "It's really my fault. I guess."

"He literally just asked me about this last weekend. Why wasn't I aware that it wasn't something you were ready for?" Brady asked. He stepped toward his sister and drew Savannah into a hug. Big-brother mode had taken over. "Liz?"

Liz just shrugged. "I mean, you *were* aware of the shit with Lucas."

He sighed. "I'm sorry. I could have forestalled this. I thought you were happy."

She wrapped her arms around her brother's torso, breathed in that old, familiar smell. And it was then that she broke down. That she finally felt like she could release all that energy. Tears flowed down her cheeks and racked sobs broke from her.

"I…was…happy," she said between choked gasps. "I was."

"Oh, Savi," Liz whispered.

Brady held her for a minute until the worst passed, and then he directed her to the couch. She plopped down, curling her feet underneath her and wiping her face with the back of her hands.

"I didn't want to cry," she muttered. "I hadn't meant to."

"Crying is fine," Liz said.

Brady came back into the room a minute later. He

passed Savannah a glass of amber liquid. "Just... knock that back."

"My older brother corrupting me," she said with a forced laugh.

"Actually, I think he corrupted me," Liz said, raising her hand.

That got a real laugh from Savannah. And then back to tears again.

"You two are so cute together," she cried.

Liz sank down to her side. "Not without some serious complications. Brady was a huge asshole for a long time."

"I'm still an asshole. Don't try to damage my reputation."

Liz smirked up at him. "Anyway, what I mean is that if you want this thing to work out with Easton, then there's still time for that to happen. You two have been together for three years, and the only complication has been Lucas and your fear of Easton going into politics."

"Hey, what's wrong with that?" Brady asked, crossing his arms.

"Everything," Liz and Savannah said in unison.

Then, they looked at each other and laughed.

"Politics ruins lives. It makes you reevaluate everything to see if it's worth it." Liz raised an eyebrow at him. "You know that better than anyone. You can't blame your sister for having qualms about subjecting the rest of her life to the same scrutiny."

"I do know that," Brady said.

"It was bad enough, growing up with it," Savannah said. She stared down into the drink she hadn't touched. Then, she took a deep breath and downed the liquid. She coughed as it burned a trail of fire down her throat. Her eyes watered. "Holy fuck."

"Good?" Brady asked.

"Excellent. I'll take another." She passed him the glass back.

"So, tell me about Lucas," Liz said when Brady disappeared.

"We kissed at his graduation. But I was blacked out and didn't remember it. He told me about it last night at the party."

"And then Easton proposed."

She nodded. "Yeah. It was…bad timing."

"So…you told him?"

"I had to. With my history with Lucas?" She shook her head. "It's a nightmare. We're just complicated. You know the story. He liked me in high school, but I didn't want to ruin our friendship. Then, we got together after graduation. But then, bam! We were split up again. He went off to Vandy and got a girlfriend. Then, he came back every summer to fuck around with me. And it happened that first summer when I was with Easton, and he found out. I promised it would never happen again."

"You haven't slept together since then, right?"

"No. But…I think if Lucas hadn't stopped us at

his apartment, we would have. I mean, how can I marry someone when this shit with Lucas never fucking ends?"

Liz raised her shoulders. "Maybe…you should see where things go with Lucas once and for all."

Savannah threw her head into her hands. "That's exactly what Easton expects me to do. He thinks that I can't be alone. He said that I lie to him and to myself."

"Lie about what?"

"Everything. I don't know. I was raised my entire life to hide my true self from the public. It seems, now, there's no difference in private."

Brady appeared then with another glass of bourbon. He passed it to Savannah before sitting in an armchair next to her.

"Excuse me for eavesdropping, but Lucas Atwood kissed you at graduation?" Brady leveled Savannah with his most big-brother stare.

"*His* graduation," Savannah corrected. "And…yeah."

"I know where he's staying. Chris and I can go straighten him out."

"Would you get out of big-brother mode for, like, one whole second?" Liz muttered with an eye roll. "You're not going to fix her problems by intimidating the guys in her life."

He sent his wife a sly smile. "I could try."

"I don't know. I don't even know if it's his fault.

Or Easton's fault. Or my fault," Savannah said, taking a sip of her drink and grimacing.

"Maybe it's no one's fault," Liz suggested.

"It's probably Lucas's fault," Brady muttered.

Liz shot him a look like she was about to smack him upside the head. He just smirked lazily like he was probably going to drag her off to bed. It was almost painful to watch their reactions to each other. Made Savannah just want to crawl back into a hole.

"Anyway," Liz said with a pointed eye roll, "what I'm saying is that it's not anyone's fault that you ended up where you are. You're all young. And you do stupid shit when you're young. You just need to decide what you want. If it's Easton, then maybe some time apart would be good. Show him that you're committed. If it's Lucas, then probably give him a heads-up that you're single."

"No," she said at once. "No, I can't tell Lucas."

"Then, isn't that your answer?" Liz asked.

"Why can't you tell Lucas?" Brady said. "I don't think for a second that you're afraid of communicating with him. You've known him since you were infants. He'd hear you out even if it wasn't what he wanted to hear."

"I just…can't," she said. "He can't know."

She set her glass down and then put her hands on her knees. Her throat bobbed as she considered Brady's words more thoroughly. It wasn't that she couldn't talk to Lucas. That had never been their problem. It had always been timing. Timing and this pull that they both felt but ignored until the whole thing snapped and they were on top of each other in the sand at Hilton Head.

She just didn't want it to look like she'd gone straight from Easton to Lucas. She couldn't even fathom doing that at this point. She felt fucked up. And worse, she didn't want Lucas to look like some kind of rebound. Some consolation prize. If she was going to decide, she didn't want it to be a snap decision.

And she knew the second that she told Lucas, coherent thought would flee her mind, and they'd end up in bed together.

The worst part of it all was that…Easton wasn't wrong.

She kept things from him on purpose. She never had to look at who she was. She'd gone from Savannah Maxwell, senator's daughter, to rebelling against that for barely a year and then right into Easton's arms. She'd never given herself the time to figure out what *she* wanted.

Even if it turned out that it wasn't either of them.

13

Empty

Going back to work Monday morning was a rare form of torture.

Savannah hadn't told anyone about the breakup, except Brady and Liz. She knew that she'd have to tell the rest of her family eventually, but right now, she couldn't even think about it without wanting to break down again.

What was worse, she woke up, wanting to text Easton. For three years, she had spoken to him almost every single day. And now...she couldn't.

He didn't want to hear from her. He wasn't available to her anymore. And that made her feel emptier and more abandoned than walking out of their place in Georgetown.

She knew the whole split was supposed to help her find herself again. Or perhaps for the first time. But all it felt like losing this huge connection. Something she hadn't even known that she relied on. Maybe that was the point.

"Girl!" Dylan cried, dashing to Savannah's side. "I am so excited for you. I've been thinking about that proposal all weekend. How fucking amazing was that?"

Savannah swallowed back the rising bile in her throat. "It was…um…"

Dylan's smile diminished only slightly. "What? Did you want something flashier? A fancy dinner? I thought proposing in front of your entire family took balls."

"It…did."

"Well, come on. Let's show everyone that ring. I got in early and was gushing to Sandra and Josephine about it."

Savannah didn't move. Not a muscle. She just froze in place. She hadn't considered that Dylan would tell other people. That she'd have to explain to more than just Dylan that she was no longer engaged. Also, that Dylan would tell people who clearly didn't even like Savannah. Thus far, they'd been nothing but rude to her.

As she was about to open her mouth, Sandra and Josephine appeared around the corner. To Savannah's surprise, they rushed right over to where she stood with Dylan. All of their frost was gone, and they actually seemed…excited to see her.

"Oh my Lord," Sandra said with a wide grin. "Let me see that diamond ring."

"Dylan was gushing about how enormous the rock is. Congratulations!" Josephine cried. She reached for Savannah's hand.

Savannah wrenched back and willed herself not to cry. She could make it through this. She could.

"What's wrong?" Dylan asked as if just finally realizing that something wasn't right.

"He, um…left me. We broke up."

Dylan's jaw hit the floor. Sandra and Josephine gasped in shock. Then, Sandra put her arm around Savannah, and Josephine patted her shoulder.

"Oh, honey, I'm so sorry," Sandra cooed.

"I cannot believe that," Josephine said.

But it was Dylan who looked thunderstruck. "I don't understand. What the fuck was he thinking?"

Savannah shook her head, unable to speak the words. But all three women took the cue and bustled her through the office. They stroked her hair and called Easton horrible names and generally tried to make her feel better. They treated her to lunch and helped her get through her massive to-do list whenever they had a moment.

It was the first time that she had ever felt welcome at her work. Who knew she just had to get dumped to be included?

"I still can't believe this," Dylan said with a shake of her dark curls as they exited the building later that day. "Had you been having problems?"

"We had one problem," Savannah confessed.

"Let me guess. Lucas?"

Savannah blushed. "Was it that obvious?"

Dylan snorted. "Yes. Absolutely. You'd have to be blind not to see it."

"Oh," she muttered.

"So, are you and Lucas…"

She shook her head once. "No. That's not happening."

"Why not? He's fine as hell."

"Besides the fact that it'd be way too soon? If something happens with Lucas, I don't want it to be a rebound. I don't want to have any doubts when I decide what the hell I'm going to do about all of this. Easton said that I need to find myself. That I'm lost and I just keep secrets and lie, which isn't wrong."

"And are you still considering getting back together with Easton?"

Savannah sighed. "I mean, yeah. We were together for three years."

"That's a lot of history to just throw away."

"It is," she whispered.

"Don't you think it makes him an ass that he just ditched you?"

"No. I mean…it was my fault."

"Is it *always* going to be your fault for the rest of your relationship? Because looking over your shoulder isn't healthy either. And if he keeps blaming you every time you're around Lucas, it's not going to work."

Savannah nodded her head. "It's kind of felt like that. But there was reason. We did kiss when I was drunk at his graduation."

Dylan arched an eyebrow. "You didn't even fuck him?"

Savannah laughed. "No."

"And you're sure you don't want to go fuck Lucas to spite Easton?"

"You're ridiculous. You know that, right?"

"No," Dylan said. "If the guy I'd just dated for three years up and left me, I would be getting some other dick, stat. Did Easton say that you were going to get back together? Did he give you a timeline? A way to prove that you'd—what did you call it?—found yourself?"

"Well, no," she whispered.

"So, he gave you some vague instructions to better yourself for him and expects you to just save yourself until he's ready for you?"

Savannah paused and looked at Dylan uncertainly. She hadn't thought about any of this in that light. She had thought she was the bad person. She was still convinced of that actually. After all, she *had* kissed Lucas. And they had slept together a couple of years ago. A slight she had been paying for practically the length of her relationship with Easton.

Not that she'd been a good person when these

things happened, but could she *ever* make that up to Easton? Was it even possible?

"Just a thought, but maybe you should decide what kind of terms *you* want to set for your relationship and stop waiting around for some guy to tell you it's okay. Be alone if you want. Fuck Lucas if you want. Only you get to choose this time, Savannah."

14

Fourth of July

Despite her conversation with Dylan about making her own choices, Savannah couldn't bring herself to talk to Lucas. Nor to message Easton. She knew that she should do both. But the more she thought about it, the more questions she had. And the swirling uncertainty made it all the more difficult.

Luckily, part of it would be handled for her over the Fourth of July weekend. Every summer since she had been a baby, her family traveled to Hilton Head with the Atwoods. It would be the opportunity that she'd been waiting for to finally have it out with Lucas.

Of course, it was also the site of their first time together…and second and third. So, it had a lot of memories attached to it. Probably not the best place to bring up her recent single status to him if she didn't want to find herself laid out in a sand dune, but she was going to do it anyway.

Her parents, as well as Brady and Liz, had flown back to Chapel Hill for the annual holiday appearances that they made for the Fourth. She'd had to work the day before and the day of. Thankfully, Clay and Andrea had waited until the last minute too, so they were all on the last flight out of town together.

A car picked them up at the airport and drove them through the darkened night to the beach house.

"Here you go, Savi," Clay said once they were parked out front. He hoisted her suitcase out of the trunk and passed it to her.

"Thanks," she whispered.

"Are you all right? You look pale."

"It's dark out. How would you even know?" she asked.

Clay shot her his best shit-eating grin. "Because I'm me."

"Clay, are you bothering your sister again? Don't you know that she just went through that hideous breakup? She's some poor, helpless creature right now."

Savannah rolled her eyes at Andrea. Leave it to Andrea to just lay it out there.

"Where you lack in tact, you make up with…" Clay said, trailing off.

"Taste? Class? Poise?" she asked, patting his cheek twice.

"Whatever you have to tell yourself, love."

Andrea winked. "We all know that I am the one who brings the class to this relationship."

"Anyway, are you actually okay?" Clay asked.

Savannah shrugged. "As good as can be expected."

"Well, I never liked him."

"What? You never liked Easton?"

"Really, Clay?" Andrea shoved him out of the way. "That's just something brothers say after their sister is hurt. Easton is an upstanding sort. He's just failed you in this regard. Try not to think on it too much."

Savannah nodded, surprised by Andrea's affection. She wasn't actually the affectionate type. And though Savannah and Andrea had butted heads for ages, she had really grown on Savannah in the last couple of years. Maybe they'd all grown up some.

But as Savannah turned to face the beach house again, her stomach knotted. She hadn't really been thinking about Easton at all. Not at this house with all her memories of Lucas in it. Lucas, who she had been preparing herself all week to tell what had happened.

As she wheeled her suitcase inside, nerves hit her fresh.

Her eyes slid over all the people who were standing in the living room at that moment. Her mother and father, still dressed to impress from their Fourth of July celebrations, were talking to the

Atwoods. Brady and Liz stood together, laughing at a joke that Chris had just made. Gigi, Clay's partner at their law firm, stood just a step away from Chris, not concealing her affection. Even little Alice was there. Not so little anymore actually. The youngest Atwood sat on her phone with her long legs crossed, looking bored out of her mind.

But...no Lucas.

She glanced backward, wondering if he had gone outside or was putting his things upstairs.

Liz approached her, still standing in the doorway, and pulled her in for a hug. "How are you holding up?"

"All right, I guess," she muttered. "Is Lucas in already?"

Liz frowned. "Oh, I thought someone had already told you. He's not coming this trip."

Savannah froze in surprise. "He's...not?"

She'd been so prepared to tell him everything... that she hadn't actually planned for him *not* being here.

"Apparently, he was called up to play in some NBA Summer League in Las Vegas for the next two weeks. So, he couldn't make it. Chris was telling us about it."

"Oh," she said softly.

"I didn't think you'd want to see him. I thought it'd be a relief."

"Yeah, a relief," she agreed. "I just had planned to

finally tell him. Figured he should hear it from me, and this would have been the first time we'd be together since it happened."

"I didn't think that you'd actually come around to telling him."

"I have to tell him at some point or else he'll find out from someone else."

"True."

"I just wanted to do it in person." Savannah sighed. She'd also wanted to get it over with. Figure out what to do about him after she saw his reaction. "I guess I'll have to wait until he gets back."

"Does that mean you two are going to finally have your shot together?"

Savannah shrugged helplessly. "I really don't know."

"Well, you don't have to decide tonight, do you? Let's just enjoy the weekend. Forget about all the drama with boys."

"That sounds like a plan to me."

"I really wish that I could have a drink," Liz said, cupping her belly. "It'll be worth it. But damn, I want one."

Savannah laughed. "I'll put my stuff away, and then I'll make you a Shirley Temple. Extra cherry. My treat."

"Woohoo," Liz said, lacking enthusiasm.

Savannah carried her suitcase up the stairs and into the bedroom she always shared with Alice. Or at least, since the age that Savannah was too old to share a room with Lucas. She changed out of her travel clothes and into her bathing suit and coverup and then met Liz down at the pool.

Clay was making drinks, which ensured they were strong as fuck. After two, Savannah was pretty sure that she shouldn't even be in the pool or hot tub. As it was, her head was spinning from the alcohol. She stepped out of the pool and reached for a towel to dry off.

"Another drink?" Clay asked.

She shook her head. "No way. That was all vodka in the last one."

Clay just shrugged. "That's the way to make them."

"We don't all have livers of steel."

"You're right. We can't all be as perfect as me."

She snorted and tossed the towel in his face. "Ass."

Her phone started buzzing on top of her pile of clothes, and she reached for it. Shock hit her in the face when she saw the name on the phone—Easton.

She picked up the phone and wandered away from the rest of her family. Her feet carried her down the steps and onto the deserted beach before she answered with her heart in her throat, "Hey."

"Hey," he said softly into the phone. "Is this…an okay time?"

"To talk?" she asked.

"Yeah."

"I guess. I'm surprised you called."

"Well, I miss you."

Her heart contracted at the words. He missed her. God, she had ached to hear those words.

"I miss you too," she whispered.

"I told myself that I wouldn't call. That I'd give you more time, but I hate it, Savannah."

"I know." She hated it too. Hated not being able to talk to him on the phone or text him about her day or see him when she got home. "I'm glad that you did."

"Have you been drinking?" he asked. "Your words sound a little slurred."

"I'm at Hilton Head with my family. Clay is playing bartender."

"Ah, right. Fourth of July weekend. Should have guessed."

Savannah paced toward the water, kicking up sand as she went. "Yep. Same time, same place. Every year."

"I remember."

"Right," she said softly. Because, of course, Easton had come with her in the past.

Easton cleared his throat as if he was debating on how to proceed and then decided to go through with it anyway. "And Lucas is there?"

Savannah froze in place a foot from the waterline. Was that why he had called? Had he known all along

138

that she'd be here, and he wanted to…check on her? It wasn't just because he missed her. It was because he was worried that she and Lucas were back together.

"Does it matter?" she asked, unable to hide the anger in her voice.

"I was just curious."

"Were you? Because it sounds like you're checking up on me."

"I'm not," he said quickly. "I just…fuck, I couldn't *not* ask. I'm going crazy, wondering if you're with him now."

Savannah's fingers curled in around the phone. "You are never going to forgive me for what happened, are you?"

"What? What do you mean?"

"You know, all this time, I've been beating myself up because I kissed Lucas when I was drunk. You were right that we needed the space to figure it out. We do need the space. Because you've never let me move on from what happened with us a couple of years ago."

"I have—"

"No, you haven't. Even now, we're broken up, and you're checking to make sure Lucas and I aren't *fucking*," she hissed. "Lucas and I have a long history. We have to be together a lot because of our parents. But we made a stupid mistake, and you've made me pay for it ever since. So, are you going to ever forgive me for that? Because I don't think that we could have a chance to get back together if you don't."

Easton was speechless for a minute on the other line. "You're right," he said finally. "I haven't gotten over it. And all the time you spend together doesn't help. I guess I have to figure out if I can do that."

"I guess you do," she said stiffly.

"I do miss you so much, Savannah. I wish it weren't like this."

She closed her eyes and tilted her head up to the stars. "Me too. But maybe you were right when you said that we needed this breakup to figure all this out."

"Yeah. I guess we both need it." He sighed into the phone. "I think I'm going to move back into the apartment. Gary's place is small, and his girlfriend just moved in. Are you still staying there?"

"No," she said softly. "I'm at Liz and Brady's place. You can have it."

"You're sure? I can find somewhere else if need be."

"It's fine," she told him with a sigh. "Someone should be staying there, and if you don't have a place, it should be you."

"I really want you to come back."

Her heart soared at the words. The words she'd wanted to hear for the last two weeks. But she couldn't go back yet. He'd left her to find herself, and she hadn't done that yet.

"I know, but…not yet."

"Fuck, this sucks."

She nodded her head. He wasn't wrong. "Tell me about it."

"I guess…I'll let you get back to your party. Have a good weekend, Savannah."

"Thanks," she muttered halfheartedly. "And, Easton?"

"Yeah?"

"Lucas isn't here."

His breath of relief was tangible. "Thank you."

"But that's the last time. We need to figure out how to move on from this."

"We'll figure it out, Savi."

She sure hoped so. Because, right now, it all felt unpredictable and painful and like a ragged piece of glass through her heart. And for the first time, she wondered if she and Easton could even make it.

15

Basketball Hearts

The weekend passed in a blur of drunkenness. Clay kept pouring. She kept drinking.

And by the time she was back to work on Monday morning, she was either still partially drunk or had the hangover of a century. After that call with Easton, there had been nothing else she wanted to do but forget everything that had happened for as long as possible.

The only good thing that had come out of the weekend was that she had gotten confirmation from Chris that he wouldn't tell Lucas that she and Easton weren't together anymore. And he'd texted over Lucas's new address in the DC area so that she could finally tell him about it all once he got home from Vegas.

"Are you sure that you don't want to go out for drinks?" Dylan asked at work almost every single day.

"We could get you a hot hook-up. Help you forget this whole disaster."

Savannah shook her head. "I'm definitely not ready for that."

"Ugh! You'll never be ready for it if you don't get out there."

She didn't want to be *out there*. That would involve talking to new people. And so far, she had no interest in going through that. Not for a long time at least.

Not when she hadn't spoken to Lucas and she still didn't really know where things stood with Easton.

But, luckily, two weeks later, Lucas finally returned from Las Vegas. She'd prepared herself the best she could for this upcoming confrontation. But she had no idea what was going to come of it.

All she knew was that they couldn't sleep together. That wouldn't be productive. It would just be them falling back into old habits. And though a good, nice marathon session sounded pretty wonderful, she wasn't going to allow it. Not when everything was so up in the air with Easton. If she was going to have a rebound, it wouldn't be Lucas Atwood. They'd known each other too long for that.

Saturday morning, she got up extra early. She put on her favorite black dress and heels, applied a fresh coat of makeup, and ran the straightener through her dark brown hair. Then, she drove over to Lucas's new apartment, which was pretty close to Brady and Liz's place.

It was a fancy, new, state-of-the-art complex that required a code to enter, which, thankfully, Chris had provided. Lucas was probably going to kill his brother for this. But she went through the gate anyway and found his place. She hopped out of the car and knocked on the front door, but no one answered.

Chris had said that Lucas had a very busy routine for the off-season to prepare for the NBA September start date. She just hadn't thought he'd be gone already at eight thirty in the morning. That was crazy early for someone who didn't normally like to rise before noon.

Savannah found her way to the connected gym and keyed in the code again to gain access. The place was deserted. Not a single person inside the entire weight room, which was good since she looked totally out of place. She followed the signs for the indoor basketball court and peeked in through the window.

Her gaze snapped to attention on the lone figure shooting hoops on the basketball court. Lucas. He was shirtless in nothing but basketball shorts and tennis shoes. His body was well-muscled with those broad shoulders and thick biceps and every naked inch of abdominal. A light sheen of sweat covered him, and Savannah's mouth watered at the sight. He looked fucking hot. So fucking hot.

This was going to be…interesting.

Still, she pushed through the door and stepped onto the court. Her heels clicked on the floor, revealing her presence. He took his last basket, hitting the three-pointer, and then turned to see who had entered the gym at this early hour.

They locked eyes. Him half-naked and chest heaving and her prim and proper and somehow completely out of her depth. This was his element. She had just entered his domain. And she was shocked at how off-balance it made her feel around him even though she had seen him play hundreds of times. Maybe thousands of times.

"Savi," he said in surprise.

"Hey, Lucas. Chris gave me your address, so I could come see you."

He arched an eyebrow. "You couldn't have just texted me for it?"

She shook her head. "I kind of wanted this to be the first time we spoke."

He picked up the basketball and set it down next to his bag. Then, he pulled out a towel and wiped his face down. "Didn't think you'd want to talk to me at all. I was giving you space, so you didn't have to."

"I was surprised that you weren't at Hilton Head. It's kind of tradition."

"It is. I assumed that you wouldn't want me there anyway. Plus, I had the Summer League."

"How was that?" With her stomach in her throat, she stepped across the court to where he was standing. She had no idea how to broach this topic. What he was going to think. What he was going to say. What he was going to do.

"Are you asking me because you care?"

She raised her eyebrows. "Why wouldn't I? You know I love basketball. It runs in our blood. You're the only traitor who went to Vandy instead of Chapel Hill."

"Ah," he said with a half-smile. "We're back to me being a traitor."

"In our families, not going to UNC is the equivalent of being a traitor."

"Oh, trust me, I heard it enough the last four years."

"Five," she corrected. "You committed to Vandy right after our junior year."

"How could I forget? You went ballistic on me," he said with a laugh. As if the memory of her anger brought a smile to his lips.

"Well, I had all these plans for us. We always went to the same school."

"You could have come to Vanderbilt too, you know?"

Her eyes rounded, and she stared at him, aghast. "Are you out of your mind? Do you know what my family would have done to me? I'm pretty sure I would have been disowned. It's Tar Heel or bust."

"Tell me about these plans for us. I didn't know you had plans for us."

"Oh, shut up. Yes, you did. You were my best friend."

"True," he said softly, glancing away. "I was."

"Am," she corrected. Her voice was pitched low. "You still are."

"Nah, it's probably Liz now."

"I've known you my whole life, Lucas. I don't think anyone else knows me like you do."

He coughed and straightened, picking up the ball and dribbling it a few times. It seemed to settle him. So he didn't have to think about what she'd said. Something to distract him.

"Well, yeah. I guess we all made choices we had to live with after high school. It changes people. Not many people stay close with the people they grew up with."

"True," she muttered. How had this gone so far askew? She had just meant to tell him. Not have a lecture on whether or not they were still best friends.

"Anyway, you asked how the Summer League was. It was great." His eyes lit up at the mention of it. "I got to play basketball for ten days straight with some of the best people in the league. It was a great start to my professional career before the season kicks off in September. Plus, Vegas."

"That sounds amazing."

She needed to say something. Get the words out. Not have them stuck to the roof of her mouth like glue. How hard could it be to let him know that

Easton had left her? That he'd walked out, and she didn't know where they stood. That she was single.

She just needed to *say it.*

Now.

"Speaking of Vegas," Lucas said, glancing back up at her, "you remember Mariah Glover, right?"

Savannah blinked a few times. She cleared her mind of the thoughts of telling him about Easton. Because...why the hell was he asking about *Mariah?*

"Your ex-girlfriend?"

"Yeah. The girl I dated freshman and some of sophomore year."

"I remember making out with you on the beach at Hilton Head for two hours while you dated her," Savannah said crisply.

"Right. Yeah. That was her."

Savannah had met Mariah exactly once freshman year of college. She was a gorgeous, busty redhead who Lucas had met at Vanderbilt. Mariah had been on the basketball dance team at the time. One weekend, when UNC basketball had been away, Savannah had flown into Nashville to see Lucas play. The encounter went about as well as expected. Which basically meant horrible. Mariah was not pleased that Savannah was there, and Mariah probably had every reason to dislike her. It had been a mutual feeling.

"Okay. Why?" Savannah asked carefully.

"Well, she's a sideline reporter now for ESPN."

Savannah's stomach flipped. That couldn't be good. "Really?"

"Yeah. I mean, she has a degree in sports broadcast, but I didn't expect to see her covering the games for the Summer League."

"She was in Vegas?"

He nodded. "Yeah, I guess she lives in DC too."

"What a…coincidence," Savannah muttered.

"It was. I had no idea she was doing sidelines or that she lived here now."

"And you two…what?"

Lucas finally looked back up at her. And she knew. She knew before he even said it.

"Well, we kind of started talking again. We spent the last two weeks together in Vegas and are going to try to pick things up again here."

Savannah felt like she was going to throw up. She'd pushed him right into someone else's arms. And how could she even blame him? Considering she'd been with Easton for the last three years and he'd just seen Easton propose. And she hadn't told him what had come next. She'd wanted to wait it out. Not to rush it. She didn't want him to think that he was some kind of rebound. And she was just as confused about her feelings. Now, she was standing here, feeling like the rug had just been pulled out from under her.

"That's…great," she managed to get out.

He laughed and shook his head. "You don't have

to lie to me. I know you two didn't get along. But I figured it was better to just try to move on, right?"

"Right," she agreed softly.

Just better to move on.

It was the smart thing for him to do.

It made perfect sense.

And yet, it felt horrid. She hadn't even come here to win him back. She'd just wanted it out in the open. So she could figure it all out from there. But now... now, she couldn't possibly tell him.

It'd be like a slap in the face. He'd just told her that he was seeing someone else. She'd look ridiculous, telling him about Easton now. He couldn't find out like this. Not as a response to him seeing Mariah again. The last thing she wanted was for him to think that she was only telling him because he was with someone else. It'd be even worse than a rebound. She'd look like she was trying to break them up. When she didn't even know what *she* wanted.

And maybe it was time to figure that out.

That was the point of this breakup, wasn't it?

"Well, I'm happy for you," she forced herself to say. "It seems that everything has lined up."

He blew out a breath. "I guess it has."

"I'm just going to..." She pointed at the exit.

"Wait, why did you come here anyway? I didn't think you wanted to talk."

"Oh," she breathed, trying to think of a response

to that. "I just wanted us to be in a better place. I didn't want us to end where we had."

"I see," he said softly. "Then, consider us in a better place."

"Good. Good."

She took a step backward. What she'd said wasn't a lie. She did want them to be in a good place. After the way things had been left at the party, she couldn't imagine a life with Lucas not in it. But that hadn't been the reason for her visit. She'd have to find another time for that.

Another lifetime perhaps.

16

Girl's Night Out

Dylan leaned over Savannah's desk and grinned devilishly. She had a pile of paperwork to get through, and after the encounter with Lucas earlier this week, she'd been focusing primarily on work. But that smile told her that Dylan had something up her sleeve.

"Can I help you?" she asked.

"So, Josephine knows a guy who works in the Business division. He invited her to this bar tonight. A bunch of the *Post* staff are going to be there. I think this is what we've been waiting for."

"We?"

Dylan arched an eyebrow. "You need to get out there. Your serious boyfriend left you, and your, like… side-piece dude has a girlfriend. It's time to have a taste of something new."

Savannah couldn't help but laugh. "Jesus, I sound like a train wreck when you discuss my life."

"Well, that's not a lie."

"Thanks," she said sarcastically.

"Come on, Sav. At least come help me find a guy even if you don't want one."

Savannah glanced away from her computer and up at Dylan. "Girl time might be nice."

"That's right. And some hot guys too."

"Maybe…some hot guys," she conceded.

Dylan squealed and hugged Savannah. "Oh, this will be so much fun."

"But just flirting."

"Whatever. I can't wait."

"Miss Gonzalez," Savannah's boss, Mr. McAllister, snapped from the door to his office. "Don't you have work to attend to?"

Dylan saluted him with a wink. "Sure thing, Rich."

Mr. McAllister sighed in exasperation. Apparently, even hard-ass bosses couldn't control Dylan Gonzalez.

"See you tonight!" Dylan crooned before returning to her desk.

Savannah just shook her head and went back to her work. But inside, she smiled and found that…she was actually excited for tonight.

———

SAVANNAH STEPPED into the dimly lit bar. Dylan had texted that she was already inside with Josephine and Sandra. She craned her neck to see if she could locate them, but the place was packed. When Dylan had said that this was a *Post* party, she hadn't thought that every person from the paper who was single would be in attendance.

She stepped around the crowd and hugged the perimeter until she saw a glimpse of Dylan's unruly curls. She sighed in relief and headed to where she was standing.

"Savannah!" Dylan cried, throwing her arms around her. "I'm already two drinks in, and you need to catch up."

Savannah laughed and let herself be escorted to the bar where they promptly did pink shots that burned all the way down. She coughed and blinked rapidly. "That was intense."

"Only the best for my girl." Dylan winked at her and then grabbed a pair of clear drinks off of the bar. "Here you go."

She took a tentative sip and winced over the sheer amount of gin in that drink. "How trashed do you want me to get?" she asked on a laugh.

"Not trashed. Just comfortably numb. Then, you'll let guys hit on you."

"Who says that I won't let guys hit on me when I'm sober?"

Dylan raised an eyebrow and said nothing.

"Fine," Savannah grumbled, taking another sip of her drink. "So, I'm supposed to help you find a guy, huh?"

Dylan grinned. "Mission accomplished. You know Brad?"

"Isn't he dating someone?"

"Not anymore. You might not like a rebound, Maxwell, but I sure as hell do."

Savannah snorted. "Oh dear Lord. Is he even supposed to be here?"

"Oh yeah, he told me he'd be drinking away his misery. It was practically an invitation."

"Practically," she drawled.

Dylan laughed, not caring an ounce that Brad probably needed a little more time to recover. Or maybe she did, and she thought a night of fun would be good for both of them. Either way, she dragged Savannah across the bar to where Brad sat with two of his friends. One wore glasses and a tweed jacket even though it was about a hundred degrees with the insane DC swamp humidity. The other was cuter with curly blond hair he kept short on the sides. He filled out his T-shirt and appreciatively looked her up and down, and best of all, she had never seen him before in her life.

Dylan plopped down next to Brad after he invited them to join, and Savannah sat down next to the T-shirt guy. He grinned at her.

"I'm Charles," he said, holding his hand out.

They shook a little awkwardly in the small space between them.

"Savannah."

"So, do you work for the *Post* like Brad?"

She nodded. "Yeah. Both Dylan and I both do. What about you?"

"Ah, not half as interesting. I work for the EPA but still working my way up. More of a paper-pusher, number-cruncher at the moment."

"Well, still, the EPA is important."

He shrugged one shoulder. "It can be. If they let us hire people and do the work. You know, it's a job."

Savannah had about a million things to say to that. She had grown up in a political family after all. She knew all about policy and the direction the EPA had taken in the last couple of years. She knew how important it all was, but it seemed that Charles didn't really want to talk about it, so she let it drop.

At that point, Dylan stood up and was dragging Brad out onto the dance floor. He must have been drunk enough to say yes. Tweed Guy and Charles shared a look.

"That's a bad idea," Tweed Guy said.

Charles shook his head. "Helen is going to kill him."

She glanced between them. "I thought he was single."

"Oh, sure," Tweed Guy said, "he's single once a month. They're toxic, but she has her claws in him."

"Jared is right. If Helen shows up, this is going to go south quick," Charles said.

"Guess she should stop breaking up with him," Savannah said bitterly.

She knew all about train-wreck relationships. She had been in one for three years with Easton. And one with Lucas for much longer. Her friends probably thought the same thing about her that Charles and Jared were thinking about Brad. It made her sad to see it all from an outsider's perspective. She didn't know Brad or his friends or his ex-girlfriend. But she knew the feelings and emotions that yo-yo'd between them.

It made her exhausted. All the years of indecision and going back and forth between these men. She didn't want to have to get drunk and talk with new guys to figure this all out. She just wanted to be happy with herself. Find what she really wanted.

And finally, she was getting some kind of grasp on what that was. It was clear that this yo-yo was *not* it. If she ever got back together with Easton, she wanted it to be the right choice, not the only choice. If she got together with Lucas, she didn't want it to be out of their continual, primal lust. The years of pent-up energy between them boiling over. She wanted it to be because they were right for each other.

Mostly, she wanted to continue her work at the *Post*. Prove to her boss that she was useful. That she could do so much more. She wanted to get promoted and eventually become the investigative journalist she'd always dreamed of. She knew that she had to climb the ladder. That her name had no bearing on why she'd gotten the job and that she was a force to be reckoned with. The paper would realize that too.

She wanted to make decisions without fear. Without wondering what these boys in her life would think or how they'd react. She might even audition for another musical. She could fit it into her schedule in the fall. She'd given that all up in college to pursue journalism like a fanatic. But maybe it was important for her to discover balance. Maybe everything she did didn't have to be delivered like a religious zealot. She could have her family and friends and journalism and still have room for hobbies. Maybe even a boyfriend if she decided on that.

For the first time in years, a calm settled over her shoulders.

Easton had been right. She needed this time to step away and figure herself out. No matter what that meant for them. Or where they ended up.

Dylan had thought bringing Savannah here would get her a one-night stand and help her move on from the boys. But in fact, she realized more acutely that she didn't need sex to help her discover what she wanted. If anything, she'd just needed to see someone else who was as much of a train wreck as her. And somehow, it all fitted together like the missing pieces of a puzzle settling into place.

Savannah leaned back against her chair, took a sip of her drink, and smiled.

Things would be okay.

Not right now. Not yet.

But eventually.

And it felt good to finally see it all so clearly.

Charles and Jared continued to talk, and Savannah was surprised to find how funny they were. She didn't want to date either of them. But it was better than waiting around for Dylan to come back with Brad.

She was shocked to find out that Jared worked for ESPN. It seemed like it would be the other way around since Jared was the smaller of the two in glasses and tweed, but apparently, he worked behind the scenes for the local network.

"How did you get into that?" Savannah asked.

"I've always loved sports. I'm just...horrible at playing them," he said with a laugh. "So, I went and got my PhD in statistics with a sports analysis focus. I had an internship with ESPN, and they kept me on. I do a lot of obscure data management. All those random stats that no one thinks about where they came from."

"Huh," she said in awe.

Way more interesting than Charles working for the EPA. At least Jared seemed passionate about it.

"Oh shit," Jared said, his eyes going round. "I didn't think she'd show."

"Who?" she asked. She looked around. "Helen?"

"No, there's this cute girl at my work. I invited her out tonight."

"She showed?" Charles asked, clearly in shock.

"Oh," Jared said on a sigh. "Looks like she brought a date."

"Sucks," Savannah muttered.

"Yeah, man. Those sideline reporters never go for the stats guys."

Jared wrinkled his nose. "I know, but..." He shrugged and didn't finish that sentence. "I'll just say hi."

He waved his hand and finally got the attention of a redhead who had just stepped through the dance floor and was now walking straight toward them.

Savannah's stomach sank. "Fuck," she whispered.

She hadn't pieced it all together. Jared worked for ESPN. The woman was a redhead sideline reporter.

"Mariah Glover," Savannah whispered.

Jared startled. "You must watch basketball."

"Sure do," she muttered as her eyes dragged to the tall guy following behind her.

The recognizable build, the shaggy, dark hair, and mesmerizing eyes. Those eyes that had found her in the crowd. That were now narrowed as he tried to figure out answers to everything at once. What she was doing there. Why she was with these guys. Where Easton was.

All the questions piled up as his eyes found hers again.

"Holy shit," Jared whispered next to Savannah. "That's Lucas Atwood. He's a five-star recruit…"

He rattled off Lucas's stats like he'd memorized them before this meeting. But Savannah could barely hear him. All she saw was her impending doom. This wasn't how she wanted him to find out. This wasn't how she wanted to tell him.

She could see the fury building in those eyes as Lucas and Mariah finally stopped in front of them.

"Well, Savannah Maxwell," Mariah said with an arched eyebrow, "funny seeing you here."

"Hello, Mariah."

Lucas's eyes narrowed further. "What are you doing here?"

"It's a *Post* party."

He looked from guy to guy and the empty space in between but said nothing.

Mariah had no such qualms. "So, where's your fiancé?"

She wielded that word like a weapon.

Savannah swallowed and moved her gaze back to Lucas's. She took a deep breath and decided it was now or never. She had decided what she wanted. No going back now.

"We broke up," she told them and waited for the fallout.

17

Boil Over

"Y ou did *what?*" Lucas asked, his voice as cold as ice.

Mariah's attention diverted to her boyfriend. Savannah could see her immediate displeasure at the way he'd asked that question. But it was Savannah he'd directed that rancor toward.

"You and your fiancé broke up?" Charles interjected, clearly not reading the situation. He tenderly placed his hand on Savannah's arm. "I'm so sorry. That's horrible."

"Yes, it is," Mariah said with none of Charles's warmth or sympathy. "How exactly did that happen?"

Savannah swallowed. "We decided we needed time apart."

"After he proposed?" Mariah asked incredulously.

"Yes, it wasn't exactly planned."

"Are you getting back together?" Lucas demanded.

She bit her lip and shrugged. "I don't know."

Jared sighed across from her. "No wonder Dylan dragged you out here. You need a drink."

Savannah didn't think drinking any more in this situation was going to be a good idea. Lucas looked as if he was going to boil over at any second. Mariah was the only thing keeping him from shaking Savannah and demanding answers. Savannah knew him too well not to see it.

Fuck, she should have just told him when she went to see him.

She had been so caught up in her own mind that she couldn't see the truth. She never should have hidden this from him. Easton had scared her into staying away from Lucas, and now, she was going to pay the price for this secret.

It was too late for her isolation to bring her the clarity she needed to know not to hide from him. Lucas was supposed to be her best friend. Whether or not they ended up dating, she had always wanted to salvage the lifelong friendship. And now…she might have fucked the whole thing up.

"I think we all need a drink," Lucas spat. He turned to Mariah. "What do you want from the bar?"

"Jack and Coke," she said softly.

He nodded once and then stormed away from the group, leaving Mariah and Savannah to stare at each other in dismay. Jared immediately stood and gestured for Mariah to join their group. Her eyes flickered to where Lucas had disappeared to, and then she finally sat down next to her colleague.

Charles and Jared seemed to be picking up on the tension between them as they tried to make small talk. But, thankfully, Dylan decided to return that minute with a rather drunk and sweaty Brad.

"Hey, girlie!" Dylan said, twirling in a circle. Her curls making a halo around her head. "Come dance with us!"

Savannah's eyes were wide. She saw her out and took it. "Restroom."

Dylan raised an eyebrow. "All right. Do we have to be girls about it?"

"Safety in numbers." Savannah grabbed Dylan by the arm and dragged her away from the uncomfortable situation.

Dylan grumbled. "If you make me lose ground with Brad, I'm going to be pissed."

"Lucas is here, and the redhead is his girlfriend."

Dylan ground to a stop. "Wait, what?"

"Keep walking," she bit out. "Apparently, Mariah knows Jared, who is friends with Brad. It's twisted fate that they just fucking found out that Easton and I broke up."

"Oh Jesus, Savannah."

"Tell me about it." She pressed forward into the restroom and leaned back against the sink. "God, this is a nightmare. I feel like I just figured everything out. Like I was in the right place, being here with you and just chilling, having a good time with friends. I didn't need a one-night stand or anything. I just wanted that time to be *me*. And now, he's *here*. And he had to figure this shit out this way."

"Yeah, that's messed up," Dylan agreed. "Keep talking. I'm going to pee."

Savannah chuckled softly and shook her head. "I'm just going to call Liz and have her pick me up."

"You're going to *leave*?" Dylan groaned from the stall.

"This is going to go from bad to ugly. It's better if I get out now rather than wait around for it to all blow up in my face. Because it will. I know it."

"Ugh, I hate this. Can't you just tell Hottie McHottie and his little ginger friend to GTFO, so you can have a good night? We can deal with it later."

Savannah sighed. She wished it were that easy. But she knew better. "I'm calling Liz."

Dylan muttered a string of four-letter words.

Savannah laughed and dialed Liz's number.

She picked up on the third ring. "Hey, Sav. What's up?"

"Please tell me that you and Brady aren't busy tonight?"

"Brady is still at the office. Some congressmen billiards and cigars something or other," Liz said. Savannah could practically see her eye roll. "How's your night out? I would literally kill someone for a margarita."

"Well, uh, Lucas showed up with his girlfriend."

"Of all the bars in DC."

"Yeah, my luck, right? So, he just found out about Easton, and he looked like he was going to kill me."

"Maybe you should talk to him. You've known him forever, Sav."

"Tonight, while he's here with Mariah? I don't think that's such a good idea. I feel like I've finally figured out what I want and who I want to be. Now, I'm dealing with this. I just wanted *one* night to enjoy myself."

Liz snorted. "I know all about that feeling."

"Could you pick me up?"

"Of course. Let me get dressed, and I'll come get you. Let's hope there isn't traffic."

"There's always traffic."

"True, true. I'll try to be quick."

Savannah hung up the phone.

Dylan came out of the stall, pouting. "I wish you wouldn't go."

"Me too. I mean, I'll probably have another forty-five minutes if traffic is shit."

"Can we just dance and forget that he's here?"

"Duh. Plus, do you really need more than another hour to get back to Brad's place?"

Dylan arched an eyebrow after she finished

washing her hands. "Of course not. Who do you think I am?"

Savannah laughed and linked arms with her again. "Okay. Let's go dance."

Dylan grinned at her and then directed them out of the restroom. They made it to the end of the hallway that led back to the bar before noticing that Lucas Atwood stood at the exit.

Dylan sighed heavily. "Should I tell him to fuck off?"

"No," Savannah muttered. "I should probably talk to him."

"But dancing, Sav."

"I'll meet you."

"Fine," Dylan grumbled. She marched right up to Lucas and pointed her finger at him. "Be nice to her. We were having a good time before you showed up, and I don't want her to be in tears again."

Lucas arched an eyebrow at Dylan's assault but said nothing. Dylan shook her head at him, gave Savannah one more forlorn look, and then disappeared. Which left them all alone.

Savannah tensed, preparing herself for what was to come. "Hey."

"How long?"

"Since he proposed," she told him.

He looked away from her, his chest heaving. "Seriously?"

"Yeah, it happened the same night. I told him that

we'd kissed at your graduation, and he ended it. Or said we needed a break. Whatever. I've been staying with Liz."

"That's why you came over."

She nodded. It was. "I was going to tell you then, but you seemed so happy about Mariah. I didn't want to make it seem like I was there to break you up."

"You think you could?" he snapped at her.

She winced and shrugged. "History repeating itself."

He ran a hand back through his shaggy hair and looked like he wanted to say more. But he held his tongue. Just let the silence stretch between them. She didn't want to be the one to break it. She didn't know why she was even still standing here. Lucas was with someone else. He had never respected that about her. She didn't want to be that person to him.

"I should get back."

Lucas turned then and pressed her back against the hallway wall. She gulped and met his hard gaze. Her heart jumped in her chest at their close proximity. At the way he loomed over her. If he were anyone else, it could be scary, but with Lucas, it just drew a pit of wild anticipation in her stomach. Something she knew she shouldn't want, but she did. She really did.

"Why do you torment me?" he asked, all calm resolve and lethal attention.

"Do I?"

"I was happy. I was moving on. I was trying to

forget you," he spat. "I didn't *want* to think about you anymore. You fucking take over my headspace. You fucking wreck my life, Savi."

She flinched at the words. "Then, be happy."

He glared, looking like he was going to punch the wall. "You think I can be happy without you?"

"I don't know, Lucas," she whispered.

"The answer is yes," he said, leaning forward so they were only inches apart. "The answer is *yes*. I can be happy with someone who is actually honest with me."

She opened her mouth to say that she'd wanted to be honest with him, but what did that even matter? She had held the truth back. She had done it on purpose. Even going as far as asking others not to tell him, so she could be the one. She understood his anger even if it stung.

"You couldn't even tell me to my face. You made me find out this way. When I was the one who had always been there. When I'd offered everything to you. And you just fucking threw it away. Then, you're sitting at a fucking bar, trying to get fucked like what we were means *nothing* to you."

"I wasn't trying to get fucked! I was just trying to find *me*." She pushed back against him. "And don't talk to me about moving on, Lucas. You're here with your girlfriend. Who you were with in Vegas and probably fucked all week. So, I don't need lectures from you about how horrible I am for being in a bar with my friend."

"That's right. I'm here with my girlfriend." He leaned back in. "And we did fuck all week in Vegas."

Her stomach tightened, and she thought she'd be sick. She felt the tears welling in her eyes, and she swore that she wouldn't let them fall.

"Are you done?" she hissed back at him. "If you're trying to hurt me, then congratulations. You did it. At least, I didn't mean to hurt you. And now, I'm thinking it was a good idea to never tell you in the first place. All we do is fight like cats and dogs. We argue and spit vitriol and claw at each other's hearts." She pushed him out of her space. "You didn't deserve to know."

She saw the anger on his face. The desire to get the upper hand. To scream that they hated each other again. Even though it was the furthest from the truth. But it was uncontrollable. Their hate as fiery and explosive as their love. She just couldn't deal with it tonight.

"Just don't," she said. "Go back to your girlfriend. Leave me out of this."

Then, she turned from Lucas, swiping the tears from her eyes, and walked away. Leaving both Easton and Lucas in the same month but finally finding herself. Bittersweet and hollow victories.

18

Confessions

"What a douchebag," Liz grumbled for the hundredth time on the drive back to her place. "*What* a *douche*bag!"

"Yeah," Savannah muttered. She stared out the window, watching DC pass by her in a blur.

"He really said that to you?"

"Yep."

"Are you sure I can't let Brady and Chris beat some sense into him?" Liz asked.

"I think he has all the sense he needs at this point."

Liz sighed. "I hate this for you. You were finally getting out there and having a good time. Then, stupid Lucas had to ruin it."

Savannah leaned her head against the window. "I should have just told him."

"You weren't in the right place for it then."

"I was never going to be in the right place to tell him. I didn't want to deal with it. With any of it. I didn't want to be broken up with. I didn't want to decide what to do about Lucas. I was avoiding everything instead of facing the reality," Savannah said, closing her eyes against the pain. "And the reality is that Easton and I are done. It's been over a month, and he's gone. Lucas is dating someone else. And I just need to be me for now."

"While I think that is a good idea, it doesn't make up for how Lucas treated you tonight."

"No," she agreed. "It doesn't."

Liz glanced over at her and then back at the road. "If he hadn't gotten back together with his ex, would you have told him that day you went to see him?"

"That was the plan."

"What do you think would have happened? Would you have gotten together finally?"

Savannah shrugged. "We'll never know."

SAVANNAH LAY BACK in the bed in Liz and Brady's guest bedroom, staring up at the ceiling as a thunderstorm raged on outside. It had hit suddenly about a half hour after she and Liz returned home. She probably should have just tried to close her eyes and let the storm lull her to sleep, but she couldn't stop replaying her argument with Lucas on repeat.

It was stupid to hate the fact that they were arguing when they'd spent the last four years doing *nothing* but arguing. But still, she hated it.

Hated the words he'd thrown at her.

Hated the way she'd reacted.

The look on his face.

The hurt he could draw out of her.

Weapons they wielded against each other as sharp as knives and cut just as deep. Born from knowing each and every trigger point. From growing up together, seeing every success and failure, every new love and heartbreak. Always being there for each other through each of them. Even when it hurt, especially when it hurt.

It was no secret to her that Lucas had fallen for her in high school. She'd been terrified of losing her best friend to look too deep into herself and see that she'd fallen for him. Instead, she flaunted every stupid, meaningless relationship in front of him in the hopes of deterring him, deterring herself. Then, when it all unraveled that night on Hilton Head Island the summer after graduation and they had sex on a dune in the sand, everything changed. For better or worse.

Because he had left for Vanderbilt with no promises. And she had gone to Chapel Hill without voicing that she wanted one.

It was the beginning of the end.

And now, they were trapped here, causing the

other pain and never asking for that promise, for fear of rejection.

She'd loved the three years that she spent with Easton. It was a different sort of love. One of mutual understanding and respect. They just fit together, built each other up. It wasn't fiery passion, but it wasn't hot, burning pain either. If there had never been a Lucas, she and Easton would already be married. He never would have had a moment to doubt her love for him.

She wouldn't be lying back in her small tank and sleeping shorts, all alone in her brother's house.

She reached for her phone and pulled up Easton's number. Maybe she should reach out. Figure out where his head was. Her finger hovered over his name on her phone. Then, she groaned and flung the phone away from her.

Desperation. That was all it would be. She'd be calling him because she was mad about Lucas. She didn't need to know where Easton's head was because it was pretty clear. She hadn't heard from him since Hilton Head, and even then, he'd only called to find out if she was with Lucas.

Being alone was so much harder than she'd thought it would be.

At some point, she must have drifted off. Because, what felt like a minute later, Liz was there, shaking her awake. "Savi."

She opened her eyes and checked the clock that read three in the morning. "What is it?"

Liz sighed. "Lucas is here."

Suddenly, she was very awake. "What? What is he doing here?"

"He wouldn't tell me. Just said he needed to talk to you. I told him to go home and talk to you in the morning, but he said he'd wait all night. What should I tell him?"

She shook her head in confusion. What the hell was he doing here? She was too curious not to know. "I'll talk to him."

"Are you sure? Brady's home. He offered to kick him out."

"No," she said, brushing sleep out of her eyes. "I'll tell him myself. Thanks for waking me up."

Liz chewed on her lip. "If he acts like an asshole again, I'm sending Brady. You don't need to keep dealing with this shit."

"You're right," she said on a yawn. "I don't."

Savannah pulled on a pair of UNC sweatpants over her too-small shorts and then stepped out of her room. Liz had gone to get Brady, who looked none too pleased. Savannah waved him off and continued to the front door. The storm had lost its temper, but rain still fell continuously. And there was Lucas, silhouetted in the doorway.

"I don't know why you're here, but you should

probably just go," she told him before she even reached his side.

He leaned forward against the doorframe. "I can't go. We need to talk."

"I think you've said everything you ever need to say to me. I'm tired. I'm angry. And I don't want to deal with this at three in the morning."

"I'm sorry," he said softly. "I don't think I've said that enough."

Savannah narrowed her eyes. "You're sorry? About what?"

"Everything." His eyes slipped to her own, and she saw the sorrow there. The apology written in the irises of his eyes more than from his tongue. "For speaking to you that way. For attacking you out of anger. For dating Mariah to get back at you."

Savannah winced at the admission. "Why are you apologizing? Why now?"

"Because I should have seen the truth when you said you'd broken up. I should have seen how hurt you were. How alone you were in it all. And I should have been there." He stepped forward into the house, clearing some of the distance between them and bringing his sharp features out of the shadow. "I should have been the one you went to and cried to. Instead of being selfish and expecting something of us. We're friends. We've always been friends. No matter how much more there is between us. But friends don't abandon each other when they're hurting."

"You were hurting too," she whispered. Her throat closing up at his words. At how much she had *missed* Lucas. Her Lucas. Her best friend.

"But I shouldn't have put that on you. It wasn't fair." He reached out and took her hand. "I've always wanted you, Savi. I shouldn't have tried to sacrifice your happiness for that."

"I don't…I don't understand how we're standing right here," she whispered.

"When I saw you sitting there with those two guys in that hot dress you were wearing, I just…lost it. Then, you told me that you and Easton had broken up, that you'd broken up and not told me, I let that anger rise to the occasion." He sighed and ran a hand back through his wild hair. "I shouldn't have done any of that. I didn't get it together until you left. Can you forgive me?"

Savannah extracted her hand from his and glanced away from him. "I don't know, Lucas. I should have told you about Easton, but you were an ass. I don't know that I want to do this right now. Shouldn't you get back to your girlfriend?"

"We broke up."

Savannah's mouth dropped open. "You…what?"

He shrugged. "It was a rebound, Savi. I tried to convince myself it was something real because I didn't want to think about you. I thought you were getting married. That you were happy. That he was what you wanted. I couldn't stand around and witness that."

"And now that I'm not, you're just going to dump Mariah?"

"Honestly, it was mutual. I think we both saw the writing on the wall when we saw you out. She agreed it was for the best."

Savannah blinked. "So…you're single."

"As are you," he said softly.

"And we're in the same city."

"We are," he agreed.

Savannah shivered at the words. At the knowledge that, for the first time in four years, they were in the same physical place and both unattached. Except that…they weren't in the same place emotionally. Savannah had just had the revelation that she didn't need anyone. Being alone was lonely, but it was better than this hot and cold. Better than the heartbreak and questions. The tempers that they both exhibited.

"I want you, Savannah," he said, bringing his hand up to her cheek and tilting her face up to his. "I can see that I hurt you. I know that you want the space to be your own person. But I'm not going to lie and say that I don't want you because I do."

She closed her eyes. "I just…I don't want it to be the same. I don't want us to keep hurting each other. I want my own life."

"I don't want it to be the same either. I want us to give this a chance. A real chance. Not fucking in secret one day and screaming at each other the next. I just want to be with you the way we should have always been together."

She leaned her cheek into his hand. "Lucas…"

"Shh," he whispered, slipping his other arm around her waist and drawing them together. "Don't think. Just do what your heart tells you. Be with me, Savannah."

She opened her eyes and stared up at his handsome face. Hearing the words she'd wanted to hear for so long. The agony that they'd caused each other slipped away. And she just saw her best friend standing there, trying to finally make everything right.

She nodded her head. "This is what I want."

A sigh escaped his perfect lips. Relief washed over his features.

And then those lips were covering hers. Claiming them for his own. She forgot everything else, just let herself dive headfirst into this moment. Into the feel of his arms around her. And it felt like coming home.

19

This Is How It Always Is

The doorbell rang.

"I got it!" Savannah yelled, dashing toward it in her high heels.

Liz snickered from the living room, and Brady stood from his seat where he'd been answering emails. He instantly went into big-brother mode. And she just needed to push Lucas out the door before Brady realized what was happening.

She wrenched it open and stilled at the sight of him. "Hey," she said breathlessly.

She was so used to seeing Lucas in basketball shorts and a T-shirt. That was his go-to outfit. But tonight, he was dressed in a charcoal suit with a baby-blue tie. It was a sharp contrast and made butterflies erupt in her stomach.

"Hey yourself," he said with a slow grin as he took in the little black dress she'd pulled out of Liz's closet.

"We should…we should go," she said hastily.

He arched an eyebrow. "In a rush?"

She tilted her head sideways, and he peered inside long enough to see Brady striding toward them.

"I can handle Brady," Lucas said.

"Well, it's your funeral."

"Lucas," Brady said, appearing at her side like an overbearing father figure.

He held his hand out, and Lucas shook it amicably.

"Good to see you, Brady. How's it going?"

"Good. Why don't you come inside, so we can have a quick chat?"

Savannah could hear Liz laughing in the other room.

"Or how about no?" Savannah said. "You've known Lucas his whole life."

"That is why I have concerns," Brady said.

Lucas laughed. "It's different with Savi."

"It'd better be."

"I'll have her back before she turns into a pumpkin," he promised with a grin.

"He's not my dad. Let's not make any promises," she said with a snort, nudging Brady out of the way. She smiled up at him. "We'll be fine."

Brady returned the look. "It's good to see you smile. Have fun."

She realized he was right. It *was* good to smile.

Really smile. And not just something she was putting on for other people...or even herself.

She kissed her brother's cheek. "I love you. See you later."

Brady watched them walk out to Lucas's awaiting Range Rover before he closed the door behind them.

"He's so protective," she grumbled.

"Hey, be glad for that. It means he cares."

"Even though he was an ass to you?"

"He wasn't an ass. He was just...Brady." Lucas shrugged and opened the door to his SUV.

"Shiny new digs," she said, admiring the car.

"Signing bonuses do come in handy."

"Is that what this is?"

She and Lucas had never really talked about the draft or anything involved. At least, not since high school when becoming a professional basketball player had been a pipe dream.

"I know they say not to buy a brand-new car and to learn how to invest your money and all that," he said with a lazy shrug, "but I couldn't help myself."

"And that," she said, poking his chest, "is how you get into financial troubles later down the line."

He snorted. "I think I'll be okay, Savi."

She realized that she hadn't moved. That she was just standing there in front of him with the door to his car open. The oppressive July heat beat down on them with so much humidity that she could practically drink the water. And yet, she took a step closer, tilted her head up to look at him, and bit her lip.

"Are you sure about this?" Savannah asked.

He didn't bullshit her. He didn't try to undercut the question she was asking. He didn't make a joke out of it. Instead, he just brought his hand up to her jaw, threaded his fingers up into her hair, and said, "I'm sure."

She swallowed, captivated by that look. "It's just... we've known each other forever."

"It's because we've known each other our entire lives that I want to make it clear that this is different."

"True. But...I don't know if it's silly."

"I told you that we were going to do this the right way. And we're doing it the right way," Lucas insisted, trailing his thumb down the column of her throat. She swallowed, her heart pulsing in response. "Which means I'm taking my girlfriend out on our first date."

She reined in the desire that rocketed through her when he touched her. "I suppose...I can't argue with that."

"That's right," he said.

A grin touched his features. He must have realized his effect on her. How her whole body leaned into him and trembled with the need for him. He bent down and roughly captured her lips against his own. She felt it in that kiss—his own lack of control. The wild thing between them that ignited upon contact. It was what made them run so hot every time they were together. It sparked fierce arguments as often as hot fucking.

She released a slow breath when he pulled back. His own breathing was hitched.

"We should…go," he said slowly. "Or else we won't make the theater."

Her eyes fluttered open. "The theater?"

He grinned. "Now, I have your attention."

"You had it a second ago."

Reluctantly, he took a step back, putting some distance between them. "As much as you make me want to ruin all my plans, I would like to take you out."

She nodded. She saw how much this meant to him. He'd wanted these real dates all the way back in high school. Then, they'd spent the next four years with this insufferable back and forth. She wouldn't let their aching, pent-up sex drive screw up their plans.

"All right." She turned from him and got in the car.

He snapped the door shut behind her and jogged around to the other side of the car. Once they were driving down the familiar DC roads with his favorite tunes playing in the car, Savannah was able to relax. One touch, one kiss awakened something between them. It was primal. And as much as she wanted to give in to it, she knew that they weren't ready. Not if this was going to last.

Lucas pulled up to the front of the Kennedy

Center in downtown DC. It was an enormous '70s-era building on the Potomac, throwing distance from the Lincoln Memorial. Savannah had been here a dozen times with her family over the years and never seemed to get over the grandeur. While some people thought that the building was outdated with its garish red and gold interior with bright pipe-like columns and glittering, circular chandeliers, Savannah still loved it. The place was attached to too many happy memories for her to see anything else.

She strode inside with Lucas at her side, her hand in the crook of his elbow. And for those moments, she felt like Cinderella going to the ball. As if this was too surreal to be true. That she and Lucas could actually have a normal evening out despite all the hateful words they'd thrown at each other over the years.

After Lucas got them both a drink, Savannah veered toward the boxes without thinking. That was where her family had sat in the past. She had always felt like a queen looking out over her subjects. A bit removed. More to be seen than to actually watch the show. She'd found it almost sad that *where* you sat mattered more than *what* you saw.

But Lucas snagged her elbow before she could take another step. "This way."

She raised an eyebrow. "But the boxes are over here."

"And I know you hate them," he smoothly told her.

"I don't...hate them."

He arched an eyebrow. "The view isn't as good. You complain the *entire* time that you can only see three-quarters of the stage. That isn't something a guy can forget. I mean...even when he is subjected to a four-hour opera."

"So...where?"

He directed her through the main double doors and down the aisle toward the orchestra. His eyes scanned their tickets before coming up on a row about twenty rows from the stage, dead center.

Savannah's eyes glittered with excitement. These were her favorite seats. She hadn't been to the theater with Lucas since she was eighteen, and somehow, he still knew that this was what she preferred. She'd been vocal about it in the past, but it seemed exactly the kind of thing that a guy who hated opera would forget.

"Thank you," she breathed, sinking into her seat. "For remembering."

He took the seat next to her and nodded to the stage. "It could have been you up there."

She snorted. "No way. I wasn't any good. I just loved it."

"Sometimes, that makes all the difference."

"It cannot make up for my lack of vocal training or my half-assed acting skills. I was good enough for small-town theater, maybe for The Triangle, but never Broadway. Hobbies can just be hobbies, you know. We don't all have to become professional basketball players."

"Let's hope not. I don't need any more competition," he said as he lazily slung an arm across the back of her chair.

Savannah relaxed against him and sipped her champagne. Soon, the rest of the theater filed inside, and the lights dimmed, announcing the beginning of the show. The room quieted, the curtain was drawn, and suddenly, she was completely engrossed in the musical version of *Aladdin*.

———

BY THE TIME INTERMISSION HIT, her cheeks hurt from smiling so much. She had forgotten how much she adored musicals, having completely devoted her life to the newspaper the last four years. She'd hardly had time to do anything else. And it felt freeing to indulge in something she had loved so much once.

She followed Lucas out of the theater during intermission and onto the outdoor terrace that overlooked the river. It was grand and beautiful, lit up by the theater behind her and the city in front of her. The Lincoln Memorial and Washington Monument were beacons in the night, standing tall against the flat DC skyline.

Carts had been wheeled out for patrons to purchase beverages or snacks. Savannah could remember begging for candy from her mother and her father indulging her despite her mother saying no. So many memories. Growing up as a politician's daughter felt like being split in two. Half her heart always in beautiful Chapel Hill and half her heart here in this political swampland.

"I'm going to get us another drink. I'll be right back," Lucas said, their lips brushing against each other before he maneuvered into the line.

She strolled toward the edge of the terrace and leaned against the railing. She had been worried about tonight, but Lucas had been beyond charming. It was amazing what they could both accomplish when they weren't screaming at each other.

She turned around and searched him out in the crowd. Her eyes falling across his broad shoulders in that well-fitted suit. The short hair he'd cut again recently that she was still getting used to after it had been long and shaggy for years. The sharp jawline and hollowed cheeks. The way his pants tailored down to his narrow hips. But it was something else. A confidence that he had, a swagger. Like he knew that everything was going to work out in his world. It was one she was familiar with and found incredibly attractive. Her blood pumped faster as her eyes crawled down his form. And his eyes skittered across to hers as if drawn like a magnet. A slow, knowing smile crossed his lips. As if he knew *exactly* what she had been thinking about.

She flushed and broke the gaze. Lucas Atwood made her want to forgo the second half and head straight home.

She was disrupted from her thoughts by an older gentleman with silver hair and a kind smile sidling up to her at the edge of the terrace.

"I know a Maxwell when I see one," he said.

Her heart stopped altogether. "Is that…so?" she asked cautiously.

"You probably don't remember me," the man said, extending a hand. "Senator Billy Chambliss. I've known your father for many years. A great man."

Billy Chambliss. Of course. Her father played golf with him. He'd come to their house in Chapel Hill a time or two. Now that she looked at him with fresh eyes, she realized she did recognize him.

"Senator Chambliss, of course," she said, shaking his hand. "It's so nice to see you."

And then Lucas materialized out of thin air at her shoulder. "Here you go."

She gratefully took the champagne from him and gestured to the man before her. "Lucas, this is Senator Chambliss from Massachusetts. He's friends with my father. Senator, this is my boyfriend, Lucas Atwood."

The two men shook hands.

Lucas smiled. "Pleasure to meet you, sir."

"Atwood you say?" Senator Chambliss said with a knowing look. "You wouldn't be Matthew Atwood's boy, would you?"

Lucas nodded. "That'd be me."

"He's a brilliant strategist, your father. He and the Maxwells go way back."

Lucas put an arm around Savannah's shoulders. "That's true. They've been friends their whole lives."

"Well, it's a real treat, running into you young folks. I don't want to take up more of your time." Senator Chambliss smiled at them both. "Tell your fathers I said hello. And that brother of yours," he said to Savannah.

"I will definitely let my father and Brady know."

The senator winked at them and then hurried back to his awaiting wife, daughter, and three proud grandchildren.

"Ready to go back inside?" Lucas asked, reaching for a hand.

For a second, she just stared up at him. Not in surprise exactly but in relief. Being a Maxwell had never been easy for her. Not like Brady, who was the perfect son, or Clay, who reveled in the notoriety. She'd wanted to be anonymous in a world where she never could be. There was no chance of it in her existence. Not with her father in politics. Definitely not now with Brady joining him in Congress.

And that interaction with Senator Chambliss, however inconsequential it had been, would have normally sent her anxiety ratcheting up. But it was clear that dealing with someone recognizing her as

Savannah Maxwell was a hell of a lot easier with Lucas.

She had always feared—however subconsciously or unconsciously—that her name meant something to other people. Just the fact that she *was* a Maxwell meant that she worried about people seeing her like that…using her for it.

It was half the reason that she'd refused any help from her father to get her a job at *The Washington Post*. Or why she frequently didn't tell people her last name for as long as possible. Or why she cringed, thinking of a Maxwell byline in the newspaper.

She knew that it was her problem and no one else's. Born from years and years of the deeply ingrained political daughter's routine. The way she was treated differently than her brothers. That made her want to hide the part of her that was known and just be *her*.

But for the first time maybe *ever*, she didn't feel like she had to hide.

Lucas hadn't even blinked an eye about her being noticed. Or about the fact that the senator also knew his father. He didn't care that his father worked for her father. Actually, nothing at all about that brief interaction had seemed to bother Lucas Atwood.

And her heart grew when she realized that she would never have to feel that way again.

20

I Know You

Savannah released Lucas's hand so that he could fit the key into the lock of his apartment door. She'd had another glass of champagne at the theater, and she promptly tipped over from tipsy and straight into giggly. Lucas found it endearing and insisted he get her home. She suggested otherwise. He hadn't resisted.

She leaned back against the wall outside of his apartment as he turned the lock and thrust the door open.

"Home sweet home," he said.

"I think I had one too many," she said, not moving from where she was standing with her heel pressed into the wall and her hands in her dark hair.

He stepped forward. His body towering over her in a way that did nothing but make heat pool in her core. "I can take care of you."

She met his gaze. It wasn't what she had thought he would say. "How exactly do you plan to take care of me?" A dirty smirk crossed her features.

His hands moved forward to cage her in, and he leaned down close to her face. "If you look at me like that, I'm a goner, Savi."

Then, he fitted his mouth to hers. Soft and exploring. Gentle yet monumental. He had touched and kissed her any number of times this evening. But this was different. This was coaxing and questioning. Like holding a bird in your hand and hoping it would fly. There was something in this kiss she had never had from him before—hope.

"We should go inside," she said when he finally pulled back.

"Yes." His breathing was uneven. A muscle flickered in his neck. Barely contained control.

He took her hand again and drew her away from the wall. She followed him into his apartment, where he promptly closed and locked the door. She had been here once before—when she came to tell him about her ended engagement. But she hadn't been inside. She'd only made it as far as the front door before going to the gym, where he basically lived anyway.

She surveyed the apartment. It was new, fresh, and modern with the space purposely sparse. As if someone had taken quite a lot of time to decorate his place so that it had that not-quite-lived-in look.

"Huh," she said, discarding her heels in the doorway and continuing inside.

"I know," he muttered. "Alice got her hands on it."

Savannah snorted. "Oh God, I guess we should be thankful this is the least of what your little sister did to your apartment. She could have gone full-blown emo on it."

"She wanted to. And I told her she couldn't try out her new interior design skills on it if she went all black and sad." Lucas shrugged. "She's actually really good for someone who is only sixteen."

"She's always been into that though," Savannah said as she took a seat on a barstool. "Don't you remember when she redecorated the Hilton Head bedroom we shared without speaking to my parents first?"

Lucas slipped out of his suit jacket and slung it across the back of a chair. "I remember the fallout for sure."

Lucas headed into the kitchen and poured her a glass of water. He slid it across the bar to her before taking out a bottle of scotch.

"I get water, and you get scotch?"

He raised an eyebrow. "You had one too many."

She huffed at him repeating back her words, but she drank the water. He was right. She didn't need to be drunk to be around Lucas. That had been the Savannah who had a boyfriend and knew she *shouldn't* be around Lucas. Not the one in his apartment, currently dating him.

"You're thinking deeply about something," he said, sipping on his scotch.

"Thanks for not being weird about Senator Chambliss approaching me."

He furrowed his brow. "Why would I have been weird about that?"

"Oh...you know."

"Do I?" he asked.

"People always recognize me...or at least, the name."

"I've known you for years. That always happens to the Maxwells. It's not weird, Savi. It's just how it is."

"Sometimes, it feels like it is."

"The last four years, people have recognized me everywhere I go because of basketball. Is that weird?"

"No," she said automatically.

"And somehow, it's different?"

She chewed on her bottom lip. "I guess not. But... it's something that you chose."

"I chose basketball, not the lack of privacy. Neither of us chose that."

"I'm just not used to people not caring when I get recognized. I get self-conscious about it. Makes me feel...other." She shrugged helplessly. "Sorry."

Something smoldered in Lucas's eyes. "Don't do that."

"What?" she asked.

"Apologize for who you are."

Lucas left his scotch on the counter as he came around to where she was seated. He tilted her chin up so that their eyes could meet. Her heart skipped a beat at the fire in that gaze. The unrelenting focus. She swallowed, and heat traveled down her body again.

His hands slipped up into her hair. "You're perfect just the way you are. And damn anyone who says otherwise."

It was those words that made her lean into his strong hands. That made her close her eyes and nuzzle against him. A sliver of herself broke open for him. Things had been so fucking hard with Lucas for so fucking long. But here, like this, always made sense. They had lived the crazy political life together practically since birth. And there was no part of her that he didn't already know.

He tilted her chin up. "Look at me, Savi."

Her eyes fluttered open, and she stared up into those rich blue orbs, still amazed they had made it to this moment. Where what they were doing wasn't illicit. Wasn't going to hurt the other in some monumental way.

"Just be here with me tonight."

She cracked a smile. "I'm here. With you."

"You're *mine*," he commanded, bending down until their lips nearly touched.

"Yes," she breathed. She arched up toward him, trying to grasp that kiss.

But he held still. All calm control. Even as his fingers fisted in her hair and his breaths came out sharp and crisp. "Tell me that you're mine."

Her breath hitched. "I'm yours, Lucas Atwood. I'm yours."

He sighed and then dropped his mouth onto hers. His tongue dipped into her mouth, tasting her sweetness. She groaned against him as he unrelentingly explored her mouth.

It hadn't been since the summer before college that they were together like this. With no barriers holding them back. And nothing between them but hot desire. And then it had been new and scary. Also, quick and hurried and furious. This was something else altogether now.

His large hands slid out of her hair and down her shoulders, taking care to touch every inch of her body. He splayed them out against her ribs, dipping his thumbs under the curves of her breasts. She gasped into his mouth at the feel of him, but he just continued downward. To her narrow waist and over her hips.

Then, he spread her legs in her short black dress, pressing them further apart until he was seated between them. Another low moan escaped her at the feel of him now pushed firm into her stomach. She could tell exactly what her words had done to him. How letting him claim her made him hard as a rock in his expensive suit pants. Her fingers groped for the button of those pants, aching to release him from the enclosure. But he was ahead of her and finally let his hands fall to her ass, where he effortlessly lifted her off of the barstool.

She wrapped her legs tightly around his waist, grinding into his body. A grunt left his lips now as he hoisted her into the air. Their kiss broke, and for a second, her dark eyes were trapped by his. By the lustful gaze reflecting back at her as she slid her wanton body against his dick, begging for release.

"Fuck," he growled. His fingers dug into her ass, trying to still her.

"Yes," she purred.

"I was going to go slow," he told her as he walked her backward to his bedroom. "I had plans to relearn every inch of your body. Make you come at least twice before I buried my cock inside you."

She whimpered. He kicked the door open.

"Now, I just fucking need you, Savi."

"I need you," she said back. "It's been…so long."

"Too long."

He tossed her backward onto his bed, and she barely had time to register that he hadn't let anyone touch this room. That all of *this* still felt like him. Like the Lucas she had always known with the comfort of his old trappings and memorabilia. This was lived in and loved. So similar to the room she had spent long days in when she was younger. But more grown-up now and decidedly more masculine.

His fingers were deftly working the buttons of his shirt. He got fed up halfway through and wrenched the thing over his head, tossing it to the ground without care. She forgot the bedroom entirely and zeroed in on that body. She'd seen every inch of those rippling abdominals and bulging biceps and the Adonis lines that led down to the other part of him that was currently bulging. But she hadn't really *looked*. Not like she was now, practically salivating.

"Dear God," she muttered. "How much *have* you been working out?"

He flicked the button on his trousers and dragged the zipper to the base. "All the fucking time. It's my job now."

She licked her lips. "It's appreciated."

He laughed, a short, breathy thing. Then, he let his pants fall to the floor next to his shirt. He was just wearing a pair of black boxer briefs that did nothing to contain him.

Savannah slid forward off the bed and hooked her fingers into the top of the briefs. He exhaled at her movement, at her surety. Then, she released his dick and saw the full length of it bob out of its restraint. Her mouth watered. They'd never had the time for this before. She was so wet that she hardly felt like they had time for much of anything but fitting his perfect cock inside of her and making them both come for days. But she knew that she wanted to know his body as he wanted to know hers.

Not just in words and looks and everyday move-
ments conveyed over years. But like this and in
earnest.

Pre-cum dotted the head of his cock as she
wrapped her hand around the base of his dick. She
leaned forward and licked it off of the tip. His entire
body shuddered in surrender at that. She thought for
an instant he was going to scoop her up and bury
himself inside her, right then and there. But then she
took him in her mouth. His head dropped back, and a
rumble filled his chest.

She rolled her tongue around the tip of him.
Then, she slid forward and forward and forward. Her
jaw opening wide, her reflexes softening so she could
take him further. Still, she didn't fit him in entirely,
and she was about to withdraw when she felt his
fingers push into her hair.

A moan left her lips, and his cock lengthened even
further. He didn't exactly hold her in place, but she
didn't move either. As if he wanted to have her there,
exactly there, for a moment longer. To feel her
wrapped all the way around him.

Then, he pulled his cock out of her mouth. She
protested, but he didn't respond. Just pushed her back
onto the bed and slid his hands under her dress. She
stilled as he reached the edges of her black thong. He
dragged it back down her legs, leaving her bare from
the waist down.

"Lucas," she groaned as his fingers inched back

up her naked flesh. So primed and ready for him. "I wanted to make you come."

"Together," he assured her as he found the hem of her dress and pulled it over her head. She hadn't bothered with a bra. "And then again."

She grinned. "Awfully sure of yourself."

He arched an eyebrow as he walked to the side table and withdrew a condom. "Should I not be?"

"Let me." She held her hand out.

He passed her the condom without a word. She tore open the material in haste and fit the small band of latex to the head of him before rolling it on him inch by inch. She could see he wanted to hurry her and be done with it. But he let her finish before crawling onto the bed after her.

"I find everything you do to be incredibly sexy," he told her as he hovered over her on the bed.

Her mind was on his fingers inching their way up her right inner thigh. "I find *that* incredibly sexy."

"This?" he asked, stroking a finger through her silken folds and coating it with her wetness.

She squirmed. "Uh-huh."

He trailed that finger up to her exposed clit, already peeking out and waiting for him. He stroked her in a slow, even circle until she was writhing underneath him.

"Fuck, Lucas." She reached for his hips, trying to drag his dick closer. To get that release she so desperately craved.

"We'll see if you're ready for me," he teased.

Then, he slipped one finger inside her. She tilted her head back at the feel of one long, thick finger probing her, spreading her wider for him. A second finger followed, finding her pussy just as inviting as the first.

"Please," she murmured. "I…can't…wait…any longer."

He chuckled softly against her lips, leisurely stroking her in and out, rubbing his thumb against her clit as she bucked against him. "You don't want to come first?"

"You said…together."

"Always together," he agreed.

He withdrew his fingers, only to fit the tip of his cock against her waiting opening. She tilted her hips up, hoping to draw him in. But he took his time, something he had never done before. Once the tip went in, a growl left his body, and then he thrust with abandon. He pushed all the way inside until their hips smacked against each other, and she cried out in a small bit of pain but so much more pleasure.

"Oh fuck, Savi," he said.

He braced himself with one hand against the bed and grasped her hip with the other before he pulled out and began to drive into her. Thrusting in and in and in as if this was all he ever wanted to do.

She reached up and pulled him down to her. Their lips and tongues and teeth met with a ferocity that was unmatched. A passion that had never fully dimmed and only resurfaced with a desperate, aching need. A moment that was unlike any of the others that had come before it. A fresh coupling. A new beginning.

"So close," she groaned into his mouth as her hips met his time and time again.

"Come for me, love," he breathed.

And then he bottomed out in her pussy, and her body gave one good shudder before exploding into a million stars. She cried out, her core tightening in rolling waves. Then Lucas hit his climax and came with a tremor and then perfect stillness. As if he'd turned to stone, except for the cum he was releasing into her.

Once the spell was broken, he dropped forward over her, panting breathlessly. Sweat beaded between them. And he kissed her swollen lips.

"You're perfect."

She smiled lazily. "You're not so bad yourself."

He snorted and nipped at her neck. Slowly, he slid off of her and went to rid himself of the condom. When he returned, he flopped down onto the bed next to her.

"Let's do that again," he said with total seriousness.

She laughed anyway. "You know I normally don't put out on the first date."

He pinched her side. "Liar."

"Hey!"

"You're so easy to tease."

She huffed, not at all upset, and let him draw her into his chest.

He ran his fingers back through her hair, and she nearly fell asleep before he spoke again, "How do you feel about black-tie events?"

"Um…good?" she croaked.

"Come with me to one?"

"What for?"

"The team is throwing a fundraiser before the season starts. We're all supposed to be there." He kissed her forehead. "You could be my plus-one."

She rose up onto her elbow and looked down into his eyes. "That sounds serious."

"I want us to be serious," he said without blinking. "I want everything."

A pleased look crossed her face. "Then, I'll go. Tell me I have time to go shopping."

He laughed and rolled her back over, pinning her between his strong arms. "You have time to go shopping." His eyes roamed to her breasts. "Now, let me reacquaint myself with the rest of your body. I don't want you to feel like I'm slacking."

"Heaven forbid," she murmured as his lips closed over her nipple, and she forgot all sense.

21

WAGs

I t had been official before. But now, it felt official.

Lucas and Savannah were a couple.

It was overwhelming, standing in the glittering ballroom with some of the tallest people she had ever met while cameras flashed blindingly. And it took a lot to make her feel overwhelmed. Growing up with her father as a politician had taken away most of her fear of these situations.

But that was politics. This was something else entirely.

This was professional basketball.

A world that she had realized, after mere seconds, she clearly did not fit into.

She should have made Lucas ask around about attire. Or done some research herself. She was kicking herself for not using those four years of journalism to help her prepare for this. What a waste.

She'd heard black tie and thought, like any other normal human being, *black tie*. Cool, careful, sophisticated. Sleek ballgowns, coifed hair, soft lips. A politician's black tie. *Not*, apparently, the black tie for the wives and girlfriends of professional basketball players.

"Are you fidgeting?" Lucas asked with a quirk of his lips.

"No," she said, stopping at once.

"I don't know this look." He arched an eyebrow. "Penny for your thoughts?"

She grinned at their catch phrase and then sighed. "I'm dressed like a politician's daughter."

"You *are* a politician's daughter."

"Well, yes. But no one told me I was supposed to dress…like that." She gestured to the extravagantly decorated women around the room. Each of them in a dress to outdo the Kardashians. Low necklines, cutout bodices, mile-high slits, and every delicate neck, wrist, and ear dripping jewels.

Lucas followed her gaze. His eyes slipped over the women of his now colleagues before coming back to her. "You look perfect, Savi."

She laughed. "You have to say that. And anyway, it's easier for you. You pull out a tux and fit in perfectly."

Though she noticed that, actually, he was dressed differently than many of the other players. Several of them were in extravagant nude suits or brightly colored jackets, short pants with loafers and no socks, multicolored, patterned bow ties. Dear Lord, they were not in Kansas anymore.

"It's just not stuffy in here. Let your hair down," he said with a wink.

Of course, her hair was *not* down. Not at all.

He laughed at the look of despair on her face. "Who knew Savannah Maxwell would be undone so easily?"

She glared at him harder. "I am not *undone*. I'm…adaptable."

"You are adaptable. You'll be fine. I'm going to make a circuit for the team." He pressed a kiss to her forehead. "Go make friends."

She straightened her back as he walked away. This was no different than any other ballroom she'd had to face. No different than the press rooms in college. Or even her office at *The Washington Post*. She was made from stronger stuff. She could endure this as well as anything else. Especially if it was for Lucas, who seemed to be glowing in the limelight of his upcoming rookie season of professional basketball. And she truly did want to see him that happy.

She'd seen nothing but that happiness the last two weeks they spent together. In fact, they spent nearly every minute together that wasn't captured by her work or his workouts. Even Liz had complained that she hardly saw her now, but she said it with a lift of her lips like she knew this newfound bliss had been hard-earned. Dylan had found it fabulous and told her to get as much dick as she could. Savannah still blushed, thinking of that conversation…even if she had been doing just that.

"Excuse me?" a woman said behind her.

She whirled around and found a stunning blonde woman in the skimpiest, tightest, most revealing dress she had ever seen. And in high heels, she barely grazed Savannah's chin.

"Yes?"

"You're Savannah, right?"

"I…am?" It came out more of a question than a comment.

"Great! Kam said that Lucas's girlfriend would be here with him. I made him ask around what your name was and what you looked like. You know how men are," she went on. "They never ask the right questions. And then we're left floundering."

Savannah laughed. She liked this woman despite herself. "I completely get that. And you…are?"

"Oh my Lord, Jesus take the wheel. I'm Tiffani, Kam's wife."

"Nice to meet you," Savannah said, racking her brain for who Kam was.

Tiffani must have recognized the look. "What am I thinking? No one else calls him Kam but me. Kamari Simpson."

"Oh!" Savannah squeaked.

She should have put two and two together. He was the star of the team. He'd moved to DC three years ago for double the money and turned the team around. But what Savannah really knew about him was that he'd played for Duke…against Brady…and thus was the enemy.

Once a Tar Heel, always a Tar Heel.

"A Blue Devil," she said with a wrinkled nose.

Tiffani cackled. "And don't we all still give him shit for it? I was born and raised in Lexington. I still never let him live down the year he beat Kentucky in the Final Four."

Savannah burst into laughter. Oh yes, she was going to get along with Tiffani just fine.

"Anyway, let me go introduce you to the girls," Tiffani said, taking Savannah by the arm as if she didn't barely scrape five feet tall.

Savannah squirreled away the names of all the wives and girlfriends she had been introduced to. She was used to having to remember specific details about people with barely any time to jot them down for an article. Her memory had to be snappy, and soon, she stood with the strikingly beautiful group of women, including Amber, Jacqui, Kelley, Leticia, and Cookie. Apparently, Cookie wasn't a nickname either.

Tiffani had sauntered off to who knew where. She seemed to be known and loved by everyone. A feat, considering the cost of getting in here had to be high…and not just in regard to wealth.

"So, how long have you been with Lucas?" Kelley asked. She was the easiest to remember since she wore a mesmerizing shade of kelly green.

Savannah bit her lip, wondering how much she should tell them. She'd always been private. But she didn't want to hide her relationship with Lucas. Not that she had to be profligate with information either. "We've known each other all our lives."

Jacqui snorted. "So, recently then?"

"No, literally, we've known each other since infancy."

Cookie nudged Kelley. "Didn't the last one say that? Theo's girl?"

"Yeah, and now, he's with Erika."

They all glanced across the room at a girl she'd met briefly with Tiffani.

"Look, no offense," Leticia said, "but rookie girlfriends don't usually last through the season."

Savannah shrugged. "There's nothing usual about me."

Kelley patted her hand. "You're real pretty and all, but it's not really what they go for. You're a bit…conservative."

"There will be a lot of women…*a lot*," Amber said, "who will be utterly shameless to get in your boyfriend's bed."

She wondered how many of *them* had been shameless to get to where they were now.

"We don't say this to be mean," Jacqui said quickly. "You seem like a nice girl."

"But nice girls get hurt here," Cookie finished.

Savannah gnawed on her bottom lip for a second. She'd only just gotten back together with Lucas. It had only been two weeks truly. But she could see perfectly clear how this life would be difficult for any woman. It hadn't been an easy thing to see him at Vanderbilt with the flocks of admirers, and they hadn't even been together then. She knew he'd be gone for games for long stretches of time. And worse, that neither of them had been faithful to their past partners. Always with each other, but still...

What if they argued one night and then he left for an away game? Would old habits win out? Would he find his ex-girlfriend in Vegas for a week while Savannah was here in DC, hammering out her journalism career?

She swallowed and released her lip, straightening her spine in the meantime. No, she couldn't think like that. Those were the words of women who had things to fear. Savannah had known Lucas her entire life. If they were going to do this for real, then she knew he would do it for real. And if it wasn't enough, then he'd let her know that too. They were in this together after all.

"Thanks for your deep concern," Savannah said

sarcastically, "but I think I can handle this on my own."

Then, she turned and strode away from those women.

And she knew that she should shake off their words as easily as she could walk away from the venomous vipers. But they clung like wet sand to her bare skin.

22

What's Owed

"Get up, or you're going to be late for work," Lucas murmured against the shell of her ear.

Savannah yawned and stretched. Her eyes were hooded as she looked up at him already in a Vanderbilt T-shirt and basketball shorts, ready for the gym. "Or you could come back to bed."

"If I come back to bed, neither of us is making it to work."

She gripped his T-shirt in her hand and pulled him down for another kiss. "Who said that's a problem?"

He laughed against her mouth. "Your boss?"

"Ugh," she grumbled. "Adulting sucks."

"The sooner you leave, the sooner you can come back."

She rolled her eyes. "I don't think it works that way."

"You've never liked mornings," he said, yanking back the covers.

She groaned. "Fine. Fine. I'm getting up, jerk."

"Don't get me wrong. I love having you in my bed," he said with a wink as she eased to a sitting position.

"You made that abundantly clear last night."

He grinned. "And the night before."

"And before that."

"Hey, we have to make up for lost time."

She glanced up at him standing over her in his bedroom. She wondered if he really meant that. Part of her said, sure, they'd wasted a lot of time being stupid. That they should have gotten together in high school instead of letting her fear of losing his friendship hamper them. They should have made promises after high school graduation when they went off to two different schools. They should have done something other than hurt each other over and over again the last four years.

But at the same time, would they be where they were right now—happy—if they'd taken another course? It might have been a circuitous, meandering route, but it was theirs. There were too many horrors in their past and fears about working through their future that it felt more like she should just live in the present with him than think about time they were making up for.

"I'm just glad you're mine," she said, reaching out and taking his hand.

"And you just got serious." He crawled on top of her on the bed, easing her back down into the fluffy pillows. "You've been getting that tone of voice ever since the banquet."

"I have not."

He stared at her with his piercing eyes. "You can't hide from me, Savi."

"I don't want to."

He searched her expression. "No second thoughts?"

"I just said that I was happy we were together," she said on a breathy laugh.

"I know. I just want to make sure we're on the same page. Communication isn't exactly our strong suit."

She nodded. She hadn't told him what the vipers had said at the banquet. And even though their words rang through her mind, she didn't whisper them to him. She knew the words he'd say to soothe her. But the truth was that neither of them knew what it'd be like this fall, and she didn't want to overanalyze something that hadn't even happened.

"We're on the same page," she told him.

He pressed his body down into her and fitted his mouth to hers. She brought her legs to either side of his hips and wrapped them around his waist, pulling him closer. He groaned deep in the back of his throat as he ground his lengthening erection against the flimsy material of her thong.

She shoved at his basketball shorts until she freed him. He was too impatient even to take off her panties. He just roughly tugged them aside and thrust deep inside of her. She arched backward, biting back a scream.

"God, yes," she whispered as he started moving.

They both knew that they didn't really have time for this. She needed to look professional for work. He needed to be in the gym already. But it didn't matter. They couldn't keep their hands off of each other. Even at the peril of her job, she still reached for his hips to drag him deeper inside her.

He growled something fierce and then gripped both of her hands in his, slamming them back down over her head. She whimpered, and her core tightened as he took control. He relentlessly pumped into her until she was shaking and everything started to go fuzzy on the edges.

"Lucas," she groaned. "Close...so close."

"Come with me."

And he hit that spot just right one more time, and she came undone. As she clamped tight around him, he bottomed out in her, his body shuddering as he hit his climax.

He bent over her and placed a soft kiss on her lips

as her insides turned to jelly. "You are going to be late to work."

She brushed her nose against his. "Worth it."

He chuckled with a shake of his head. "Indeed."

———

SAVANNAH MANAGED to only be five minutes late, but she didn't regret the shower she'd indulged in one bit. Coming to work smelling like sex was probably worse than being five minutes late. Even enduring the tongue-lashing her boss gave her for the inconvenience. But she worked twice as fast as all of his prior assistants, so he let it go pretty quickly.

She'd been working so diligently, she hadn't even noticed the time until Dylan appeared at her desk.

"Hey there. Are we still doing lunch?"

Savannah glanced up. "Christ, is it already noon?"

"Yep. Sure is. I know you must not be aware because of your sex daze."

She rolled her eyes.

"Or is it the late-night gala events for the basket-ball team?" Dylan pulled out her phone and started scrolling.

"It is neither."

"Look at this shit that I found this morning." She handed the phone to Savannah, who warily took it.

She looked down at the article buried in the

Sports section, which included a write-up on the basketball gala she had attended. Including a full spread of the team and a few individual shots of the players with their girls. She recognized Kamari and Tiffani together, looking like a ridiculously matched set. And then her eyes rounded when the picture at the bottom was *her*.

"Oh my God," she whispered.

"Yeah. That's you, girl!"

"I mean...I knew that Lucas and I were photographed together, but shit..." She read the section, and her frown deepened.

Rookie Lucas Atwood with girlfriend, Savannah Maxwell, daughter to Senator Jeff Maxwell.

"Ugh! They know who I am now."

"Well, duh."

"I've worked pretty hard to not have my name or picture attached to my father like that."

Dylan shrugged. "It's who you are. Just own it."

Except it wasn't who she was. Or she'd worked her whole life to be *more* than just Senator Maxwell's daughter. And now, she was Lucas Atwood's girlfriend. It was as if she were always just a product of some guy instead of a person in her own right. Frustrating in a way that she couldn't describe to someone who had never had to endure it.

"I don't know," Savannah said instead of explaining. It was easier that way. She handed the phone back.

"Ohhh," Dylan cooed as they headed out of the building. "Do you think Easton is going to see this?"

Savannah stopped in front of the elevator. "Uh…I don't know. It's kind of obscure. I wouldn't have even seen it if you hadn't shown it to me."

"Is he a sports guy?"

She nodded. "He coached tennis and loves basketball. But that doesn't mean he reads the Sports section of the newspaper…right?"

Dylan shrugged. "I don't know, but I would love to be a fly on the wall if he sees it. He's going to lose his shit."

"You're probably right." Savannah frowned. "God, I am not looking forward to *that* conversation."

"He doesn't know you're with Lucas, does he?"

"Ha! No. I'm not telling him that. Not after what he said when we broke up."

"Are you two still talking?"

Savannah shook her head. "I haven't heard from him in weeks. I don't even know what he's doing. It's…kind of easier that way."

"Do you miss him?" Dylan asked, prying.

"I don't know. We were together for three years. So, I think about him. How could I not?"

"But not since you got your new man."

Savannah laughed. "I guess so."

"That's good. That's healthy." Dylan tilted her head to the right. "I was thinking Thai?"

"I'm game."

Just then, her phone buzzed in her purse. Savannah tensed, anticipating the text from Easton. She knew it was coming. She wasn't lucky enough to avoid it.

But when she checked her phone, it was just from Lucas.

Got called in for an interview tonight. Going to be home late. Will let you know when I'm on my way back.

She jotted out a quick response.

Sounds good. Miss you.

Miss you too.

She grinned giddily at the text before putting her phone away and trying to let it all roll off her shoulders. She was happy. She was with Lucas. Maybe Easton wouldn't even see the picture. Maybe he'd wouldn't care. Maybe he'd already moved on too. Though a part of her twinged at that thought. But she couldn't have it both ways. And she was finally happy with the boy she'd always wanted. Whatever Easton was doing…was none of her business.

———

"LET me know if you get that text message," Dylan said with a wink.

"I've been lucky," Savannah said as they left their floor and headed for the elevators at the end of the day. "I think I might be in the clear."

She was amazed that Easton hadn't texted her.

But also relieved. Not that he'd be happy to know she was with Lucas, but this seemed like a good sign. He'd been a bit out of sight, out of mind the last couple of weeks. And that was a good thing for her relationship with Lucas. She'd like to keep it that way.

"Well, I'm dying to hear more of the Savannah saga."

"You're the worst. You know that, right?"

"Obviously," Dylan said with a laugh as they strode across the lobby. "And hey, maybe this weekend we can actually hang out. You can even bring Lucas. That is, if you're not too busy fucking all weekend."

Savannah just shook her head. "You're ridiculous."

"Love you! See you tomorrow."

"Bye, Dylan."

They exited out into the muggy August air. She immediately reached for a hair tie and pulled her long, dark hair off of her neck. She was not looking forward to the Metro ride back to Liz and Brady's. For a split second, she missed her place in Georgetown. She'd have to find her own place here soon. She knew she was cramping her brother's style, but she wasn't ready to sign a new lease. Or make any decisions about her life at all. It just finally felt like she was getting back on track.

With a sigh, she headed toward the nearest Metro station. She'd only gone a half-dozen feet when she heard her name being called behind her. She turned around in confusion and then froze.

"Easton?" she muttered.

Then, there he was. Jogging to catch up to her. His blond hair, somehow even brighter than she remembered. And those eyes bold and staring straight through her. He was in a slick black suit. His blue tie perfect, held in place by a tie clip she'd given him when he first got the job with Brady. He looked...good.

Her heart skipped at the sight of him. Two months. It had been two months since she saw him. Now...here he was. Right in front of her. And she remembered all three years they'd spent together. The good and bad and the life she'd envisioned for them.

"Savannah," he said when he finally reached her. "You look beautiful."

She stumbled out of her vision and took a step back. "What...what are you doing here?"

"I left work early to try to catch you."

"Why?" she asked.

"Because I...I fucked up." He looked so earnest when he said it. He ran a hand back through his hair. "I can't believe I fucked this up so bad."

She reflexively narrowed her eyes. "Is this about the article?"

His brows rose in confusion. "What article?"

But she didn't buy it. She hadn't heard from him in weeks. He'd dropped off the face of the planet.

She'd assumed…they were over. And now, he was here? On the day that there was an article about her and Lucas together in the paper?

"The article in the paper. With me and Lucas."

Easton's eyes shuttered at the mention of Lucas. "I…didn't see anything about you and Lucas."

And she searched those eyes, that perfect face, the one she had loved for so long. She tried to see the guile in them. The reason to let her anger rise, so she could walk away from him without looking back.

But it just wasn't there.

How could it not be there?

"So…you just…came on your own?" she whispered. "Two months later?"

"I…I waited for you," Easton said. "I thought that if I gave you your space, then you'd figure out what you needed to figure out. I thought you'd come back. That I wouldn't have to live in our apartment in Georgetown alone anymore. But then I realized I was an idiot. And if I wanted to make it work, then I would have to come back for you. So, I'm here." He took a step toward her, clearing the distance. "I'm here because I love you. I've always loved you. I want to spend my life with you. Have a forever with you. You're it for me. You're the one."

A shiver ran down her back, and goose bumps broke out over her flesh at those words. The ones she'd longed to hear him say all those nights she waited for him.

"Easton...I...I don't know."

"Please." He reached out for her, taking her hand in his. When she didn't immediately jerk away, he drew her a step closer. "I'm so sorry for what we went through. You were right. I needed to realize that I could forgive you and move on from what had happened. And I know that this is what I want. You're the one I want."

She opened her mouth and then closed it. She had no idea what to say to that. She had never in a million years expected this conversation. Anger she had anticipated. But love...she didn't even know where to begin.

"Can we just go somewhere and talk?" he asked.

"I'm not sure that's a good idea."

"We were together for three years, Savannah," he said softly. "Let me take you to dinner or coffee or something. I feel like we owe each other a conversation."

She found herself nodding despite herself. It *had* been three years. And they had ended in such a horrible place. A broken engagement. Hate-filled words. One conversation could be okay.

"Coffee," she finally said.

He smiled brilliantly, lighting up the street all around him. "You won't regret this."

"It's not...we're not..."

"I know," he said automatically. "But...we should talk, right?"

She slowly nodded again. "Right."

"Come on. I know you love that place two blocks over. A flat white?"

She could do nothing but nod as she walked with him to have a long, overdue conversation.

23

Cake

Savannah felt like a wrung-out dish towel.

Seeing Easton had been a lot harder than she had thought it would be. Talking to him, seeing that smile, feeling the three years they'd had together slide back over her so easily. The whole thing had made her heart ache.

And she knew that feeling wasn't over. Because now, she had to see Lucas. She wasn't dumb enough to think he would be pleased by the latest news. She just hoped it was like taking a Band-Aid off—quick and painless.

She knocked twice at his door and heard him yell, "Door's open!"

She turned the knob and walked inside. Lucas was just peeling his suit jacket off and loosening the black-and-gold-striped tie. To Savannah, Lucas in a suit was the equivalent of her standing around in lingerie.

Sexy as hell.

His eyes locked on to her as she entered the room, and his smile lit up. For just that second, she imagined not telling him about the conversation she'd had with Easton. How much easier it would be to say nothing and pretend he hadn't begged her to come back.

But that wasn't the bargain. That wasn't the deal she'd made with herself for this relationship. She wanted a clean slate. Lucas had wanted it to be different. Which meant she had to tell him. No matter how it would hurt him to hear it.

"Hey," she said with a half-smile. She closed the door behind her and walked over to him, depositing her keys in a basket of knickknacks nearby.

He reached out for her, wrapping an arm around her waist and dropping his lips down to meet hers. "Hey yourself."

"How was your interview?" she asked, pulling back just a step.

"Everything went great. Charmed the shit out of them," he said, lighting up even more. He tossed his tie on top of the suit jacket he'd slung on the back of the kitchen chair.

"That's great! I knew they'd love you."

"Yeah, well, new team, new experience. You never know," he said with that same damn smile. "They're having me out for some TV spots this weekend. Going to finally get to put the uniform on."

"I can't wait to see you in uniform," she told him honestly.

"Well, maybe if you're lucky, I'll let you come out and watch." He loosened the top two buttons of his shirt.

She laughed softly. How the hell was she going to tell him now? She wanted to rip his clothes off and ride him right here on the kitchen counter. Forget about the last hour. But it wouldn't solve anything, and he'd be more hurt later.

Her eyes flickered away from him as she steeled herself for what she knew she had to do.

But Lucas knew her too well. He must have seen something like anguish in her expression. Because he paused his relentless flirting and tilted her chin up to meet his gaze. "What's going on with you? Work suck today? Your boss wasn't pissed that you were late, was he?"

"No. Well, yes, he was," she amended with a wince. "But can we talk for a minute?"

His smile faltered. "That's never a good opener."

"It's not…bad."

"But it's not good?"

She frowned. And shook her head once. It wasn't good. Not for them. Lucas was not going to take this well, and she could hardly blame him.

He crossed his arms, taking a defensive position. As if he was preparing himself for the worst. And she hated that she brought that out in him. That they couldn't just trust each other because they hadn't for so long. It had never been clearer in his stance.

"Well?"

Savannah swallowed. "I saw Easton today."

Lucas went stock-still. His jaw locked and eyes hardened. He was a statue of bristling outrage. Trying so desperately to hold it in that he could barely contain his wrath in his next word. "Why?"

"He…he came to see me after work. He wanted to talk."

"And did you?"

She nodded slowly. "We'd been together for three years, Lucas. Our breakup was horrible. I was a total wreck. He was a wreck. He's still living in our Georgetown place. The whole thing has been a nightmare."

"It hasn't felt like a nightmare the last two weeks."

"No, this isn't about us."

"Isn't it?"

She sighed. "It isn't. When Easton and I broke up, he said he wanted me to find myself because I was lying to everyone, especially myself."

Lucas snorted. "Of course he did."

"He wasn't wrong," she told him. "I was lying to everyone. I didn't tell him about you or the audition. I couldn't share every part of myself with him. And I had such strong feelings for you, but I couldn't admit that to you, so all we did was argue. And I lied to myself about all of it, that I was doing it for the right reasons. But I wasn't. I was doing it because it was easier for me. And that's why I'm telling you that I saw Easton. Because I don't want to lie to you."

"You haven't lied to me, Savannah. But I don't understand why the hell you'd even talk to him. Like, what could you *possibly* have to say to each other?"

"When we broke up, it didn't end like, *This is over forever*. It was more…a break to see if we could have some time away from our problems."

"I'm sure he said such nice things about you being with me."

She winced again. "Well, when we broke up, he said if I landed in your arms, then I would have proven his point. That I'd choose convenience over working on myself."

"Jesus fucking Christ, Savannah. That is *not* what's happening here. Can't you see he's manipulating you?"

"Yes," she told him, tipping her chin up. "He was. But we ended in a weird place, and I felt like I owed him at least a conversation."

Lucas's eyes narrowed. "You don't *owe him* a goddamn thing, Savannah."

"It was important to me," she admitted. She hadn't realized how important it was until she'd seen him walking toward her after work. The knot in her chest had loosened, and she'd realized that she needed that talk as much as Easton had. "I wanted to clear the air."

He shook his head. One second away from an

outburst. Raw energy coiled around him, radiating in waves. As if, at any moment, he might combust. "This is fucking ridiculous mind games," he growled. "You don't owe him anything. You don't have to clear the air. You don't have to fucking see him. All that does is fuck everything up!"

Savannah took a step back at his anger. She'd known he'd be angry. Even expected it. They'd had epic arguments in the past. But she really didn't want this to go there. She just wanted him to understand.

"Lucas, please," she murmured. "You were the one who said we didn't have good communication. I could have hidden this. I didn't have to tell you what had happened. Or that he had come to see me. I could have lied. But instead, I'm standing here, telling you the truth."

A shudder ran through him as he tried to rein in his mounting anger. "Fine. What did you and Easton so desperately have to talk about?"

She opened her mouth to respond, but he just held his hand up.

"Wait, let me guess," he drawled. "He wants to get back together."

"He...does," she said warily.

Lucas laughed, but it wasn't filled with humor. It sounded hollow, as if he'd known this moment was coming and hated that he'd been right. "Oh, I bet he said that he loved you and he'd messed it up. That he wants to make it up to you. That you're the only one for him. Despite the fact that he didn't give a shit about that until he saw the picture of the two of us in the paper. How fucking convenient."

She bit her lip. Lucas was right on point. Easton had said those things. Except for the picture. She'd had the same thought, and she couldn't blame him for believing that too. But it wasn't true.

"Yes…he said all of those things. But he hadn't seen the article. It wasn't like that."

Lucas stared back at her like she was the most gullible idiot on the planet. He took two steps forward and put his hands on her shoulders. "Please, *please*, tell me you don't believe that."

"He was telling the truth," she told him.

He slowly shook his head back and forth. "Savannah, the timing is too goddamn convenient. He saw that you were with me after he *told you* not to be with me and fucking blew a gasket. You have to see that he would do anything to keep us apart. He'd rather get back together with you, the woman he despises for cheating on him, than let us be happy."

"He doesn't *despise* me." How could he even say that?

"A part of him does. And that part of him that hates you for what you did to him also hates himself. The two of you could never repair that. Not in a million years. But still, he'd rather endure that with you every day—that untreatable pain—than see you with me, his enemy."

Savannah brushed his hands off of her shoulders. "That is *not* what's happening here. He was not there because of us. And if you had seen his face, then you'd know that he hadn't seen the article."

Lucas threw his hands up in the air and cursed colorfully. "I must be out of my fucking mind. Why do I fucking do this to myself? Easton swoops in and says the most convenient fucking thing in the world, and you actually believe his stupidity." He whirled back to face her. "Don't you understand that he would say anything—*anything*—to get back together with you?"

"Just like you did?" she snapped back, her own anger rising at his accusations.

"Yes!"

She jolted at his outrage. The real anger and... fear on his face.

"Yes, I would. And I fucking have, Savannah. To get you, I'd do anything. That's how I know exactly what the fuck Easton is doing."

Savannah bristled at his words. The way he talked about it made it seem like both guys were just conniving jackasses set out to manipulate her. And she was tired of being manipulated. She'd thought they were past that. That Lucas saw what they had as real and not something he had to do or say just to keep her.

"So then, how are you any better than Easton?"

Lucas shook his head. "Fuck that, Savi. If you can't see it, then how the fuck can I explain it to you?"

"You just *said* that you'd do or say anything to get me. That means lying and manipulating me! That means doing the things you just accused Easton of. All of this is so fucking frustrating. Why can't it be easy?"

"Because love isn't easy!" he roared. "It's hard fucking work."

"What happens when the work is too hard?" she demanded. "What happens when you're away for a game and there are thousands of girls throwing themselves at you? And I'm home, working on my journalism career? What happens then?"

Lucas blinked as if he had no idea what she was talking about. "What? Where is this coming from?"

"The girls I met at the banquet said that rookie girlfriends don't make it."

"So?"

"They *never* make it, Lucas! Even the ones who have been together for years," she shouted. "You guys always end up fucking someone else on the road! That this business isn't meant for nice girls. Girls like me."

"I'm not going to do that," he said automatically.

She snorted. God, how she wanted to believe him. "With our history? All we have ever done is cheat on other people to be together. How the fuck do we know that it's not going to happen in reverse now that we're a couple?"

"So, you don't even want to try?" His eyes were wide with alarm and outrage.

"I didn't say that," she groaned.

"Then, what *are* you saying?" he demanded.

"Nothing! I just want us to talk about this." She buried her face in her hands. This had gotten completely out of control. Just like all their past arguments.

"Saying that means that you think there's something for us to talk about."

He paced away from her and then back. She flipped her hair back to watch him with wary eyes.

"Do you think I'm going to go out on the road and fuck some groupies?"

"Do you think that I'm going to let Easton manipulate me?"

Lucas stared at her. They were in a standoff. Because the truth was that both of them didn't believe that fact, but they didn't *not* believe it either. It was a fear. A deeply ingrained fear. That neither of them could shake.

"I think he's manipulating you right now." Something hardened in Lucas's face. "That asshole knows exactly what he's doing. And I think it's time that he and I finally had it out."

"What does that mean?"

Lucas grabbed his car keys. "It means, he put this shit in your head. He came back, saying he loves you and wants to be with you. Once again, I'm the bad guy. Even though he's trying to fuck up what we have. So now, I think it's time that we talked."

He pushed past her toward the door.

"Lucas, wait, please!" She reached for him, but he just wrenched away. "Just stay and talk to me. If you go see Easton, you're just going to end up fighting. This isn't a good idea."

"It's the only idea," he said as he stormed out the door.

"Lucas, stop!" she called after him, but he was already halfway to his parked Range Rover.

Savannah put her hands into her hair and wanted to scream. How the hell had all of this gone so wrong? She'd just wanted to have an honest conversation. Not scream at each other about all their insecurities. And he hadn't even fucking given her a chance to explain what had even really happened with Easton.

Fear shot through her. Because Lucas and Easton in the same place spelled disaster. One of them would kill the other.

Fuck, fuck, fuck.

She couldn't let this happen.

Savannah dashed back for her keys and then hurried out into the night after him.

24

Lucas

Twenty-two years.

That was how long he'd known Savannah Maxwell.

And he'd been in love with her for nearly every single one of them.

They'd had their ups and downs. And for the last four years, it felt like, ninety-five percent of the time, it was hard-hitting lows. But now that he finally had her, there was no fucking way he was going to let her get away. Easton could go fuck himself for all he cared. He couldn't have her back. He had been stupid enough to let her go, and now, it was too late.

He'd never liked Easton. Not that he'd expected to like any guy that Savannah dated. But this was personal. He wasn't going to stand by and let Easton try to get in the way.

Savannah was end game. She always had been. It had just taken them too damn long to figure it out.

And he was going to make sure Easton knew that loud and clear.

No more surprise fucking visits at work.

No more deep, heartfelt conversations about his feelings.

No more *owing him* jack fucking shit.

He didn't care how he drilled that into Easton's head, but he'd get the fucking picture one way or another.

Lucas circled the apartment a half-dozen times before he found a parking spot in Georgetown. The city was so fucking packed at this hour. Everyone was already home from work or out for dinner. The lack of parking only made him more irritated. Eventually, he found a spot for his Range Rover a few blocks away. He parallel-parked and then jogged the scant blocks to the apartment building.

He was glad that he still had the address saved from when Savannah had first moved in. Though he'd never been here, he could see why she had wanted to live in this area despite the horrible parking situation. Georgetown was nice and trendy, filled with brown-stones and brick-lined walkways. There were shops on every corner with pedestrians milling about and cyclists hurrying past the crowded streets. The area felt just like something Savannah would want.

And if she hadn't moved in with Easton over here,

Lucas might have even considered the move for her. Even if it was too far from his work to justify it.

He shook his head in frustration. Another thing that Easton had ruined. He'd hated the thought of Savannah and Easton moving in together. Three years together at UNC, and they'd never moved in. He'd taken it as a sign that she wasn't that serious. But then the Georgetown apartment and straight to a fucking ring. Yeah, he needed to cut this shit to the quick.

Lucas walked into the landing and then up the three flights of stairs and down the hall. He stopped in front of the apartment and banged on the door without preamble. He heard Easton shuffling around inside.

"Just a minute," he called from the other side.

A lock slid out of place. The handle turned. And there he was.

Easton looked like shit.

He looked like even worse shit when he realized Lucas was standing there.

Good.

Easton's eyes narrowed. "What do you want?"

"I think it's about time we talked," Lucas said, pushing the door open wider and entering the apartment, uninvited.

It was fucking tiny. He could practically take in the whole place in a glance. It had Savannah written all over it. She had clearly decorated every inch of the apartment. It only pissed him off more that all of her stuff was still here. They would need to remedy that.

"I have nothing to say to you," Easton spat, continuing to hold the door open pointedly. "Now, get the fuck out of my apartment."

"We have unfinished business." Lucas returned his attention to Easton, who looked about ready to launch himself at Lucas for daring to show up today.

"I'll repeat myself. Get the fuck out of my apartment."

Lucas glared. "No."

"What the fuck do you want? You already stole my girlfriend, the love of my life, and the woman I planned to marry. Is that not enough for you?"

"It's not going to be enough until you stop coming around and bothering her."

"That's real rich, coming from you. All you did was pop up out of thin air when we were together."

"Yeah, but I'm not like you," Lucas said menacingly. "I won't stand by and watch you fuck this up for me."

"I don't give a shit about you. I only care about Savannah. And whether or not she's happy. Do you think she would have gone out with me if she was so very happy with you?"

"You fucking tricked her into thinking that she owed you something!" Lucas shouted. His blood was boiling over. He clenched his hands into fists and had to remind himself that Easton wasn't worth assault charges. No matter how fucking much he wanted to bury his fist in Easton's face.

"She did owe me something," Easton said icily. "We owed it to each other."

"She owes you nothing."

Easton shrugged. "That's not what Savannah thought. And anyway, I don't know why you fucking care."

"Savannah is the only person who has ever meant anything to me. You're trying to get in the way, and I won't let that happen."

"Well, get in line, buddy." Easton glared back at him. "Savannah was the only person who meant anything to me, too, and it didn't stop you from sleeping with her when we were together."

"It takes two people for that, *buddy*."

Easton gritted his teeth. "You jerk her around like she's a toy doll and then act like she's as precious as a diamond to you. While I'm the one who has treated her like a diamond all along and had to watch her get slung like a yo-yo from your bullshit."

"I'm not jerking her around. You can think whatever you want about us. I really don't fucking care. But you and I probably should have done this a long time ago."

"Yeah, we probably should have. So I could have said the same fucking thing to you," he snapped. "Since you were the bastard who kept coming on to her when we were together."

"I don't care what happened in the past. I care what is happening in the present." He stepped up until he was in Easton's face. Lucas stood a good two to three inches taller than Easton when he looked down at him over the bridge of his nose. "I don't want to have to say this again: stay the fuck away from her."

Easton laughed, something deeply broken. "Or what?"

Lucas flexed his hands. He was itching to punch him. To silence his fucking mouth and wipe that shit-eating grin off of his face. Lucas ached deep within himself to end this right here, right now.

And the old Lucas would have.

He wouldn't have thought twice about the consequences of his actions. But now, with everything he had on the line, he realized…Easton wasn't worth it. And worse, Easton was just goading him. Easton wanted him to step out of line. Easton wanted to see Lucas do something stupid. Something he could use to show Savannah how she had chosen incorrectly.

But he wasn't that guy anymore.

He took a step back.

He wouldn't give in to this.

"I said what I had to say," Lucas said finally. "We're done here."

"Why the fuck did you even come then?" Easton asked, prowling for a fight. A fight that Lucas knew Easton could never win. "You just wanted to rub it in my face that you won? Is that it? You wanted to hear me say that you fucking won?"

Lucas narrowed his eyes. "What?"

"Savannah said she chose you," Easton ground out. He crossed his arms over his chest. "She and I are over. Congratu-fucking-lations."

Lucas shook his head in confusion.

Why hadn't she said anything? She'd presented what had happened but not the full story. No…this wasn't her fault. He hadn't let her explain herself. He'd just made assumptions about what the fuck he thought had happened. Then, they'd screamed at each other until he stormed out.

"Fuck," he whispered before turning hastily toward the door. "This was a mistake."

"Finally," Easton grumbled. "Good riddance."

Lucas nodded once and then dashed through the door. He was halfway down the hallway when he saw a figure emerge up the stairs. He slowed and then came to a step at the landing as Savannah materialized before him.

"Savi," he breathed.

She sighed. "What did you do?"

"I'm sorry I ran out. I'm sorry for coming here. For not letting you tell me the truth without getting angry."

She held up her hand. "Please, stop."

He fell silent. But God, he'd fucked up. Really fucked up. And he needed to make this right. Something had taken over his body—an instinct to protect what was his. And it was fucking terrifying how easily he'd given in to it. How close he'd come to snapping and punching Easton. To ruining this all.

And for no reason at all. Because Savannah had chosen him. She'd turned Easton down. And he was the idiot who hadn't even let her tell him that.

"I need to talk to Easton," she said carefully. "Apologize to him for all of this."

Lucas winced. "I could…"

"No," she said quickly. Her calm was almost more unnerving than her anger. "I'm sure he doesn't want to see you. Can you just wait for me downstairs, so we can talk?"

"Yeah." He nodded. "Sure."

"Good. I'll be right back."

Then, he had to watch her walk past him and into the apartment she'd shared with Easton. He gritted his teeth, hating that sight. But he'd earned this. And as he trudged down the stairs, he realized he had to find a way to fix this…or she might very well leave him too.

25

The Last Good-Bye

Savannah took a deep breath before walking back into the apartment that had once belonged to her. It still felt like hers. She'd never come back and gutted the place. A part of her had held on hope for so long that they'd work it out. That she'd move back in. Then, once she and Lucas had reconciled, she had just given up on it. Put it in the past. She had everything that really mattered to her. The rest was just fluff, and Easton could decide what to do with it all.

Easton's head snapped up at her entrance. "Savannah!"

"Hey, are you okay?"

He laughed despairingly. "I'm assuming you're not here to get back together?"

She shook her head once. "No, I'm not."

"I didn't think so." Easton rose to his feet with a sigh.

He stood and opened his palm to reveal what was inside. It was the diamond ring. The one he'd proposed with.

A lump formed in her throat. She didn't know what to say. Maybe there was nothing to say.

"I thought you'd wear this again someday," he admitted. "Kept it, of course, hoping. But I was an idiot and saw it all too late."

"I'm sorry," she said and meant it. Because she had done horrible things to bring them to this moment...and so had he. "Also for Lucas's behavior."

Easton closed his fist over the diamond again. "You really want to choose *him*?"

She bit her lip. She didn't want to have this conversation with Easton again either. "I know that you'll never understand."

"No, I won't. Especially not after he burst in here and threatened me."

Savannah sighed. "I don't know what he said. But I'm sorry that he came at all. That you got dragged back into this. You don't deserve that. I really do mean what I said earlier today...that I hope you find someone great for you."

"You were great for me," he said hoarsely.

"When we worked, we were great. But we didn't always work."

"And you think you work with *him*? Good luck with that."

"I know that you don't mean that sincerely, but… thank you anyway. I really do wish you the best."

"I know, Savannah," he said on a sigh. "I just wish your best wasn't with him."

She stepped forward one more time and wrapped her arms around his neck. He stalled for a few seconds before pulling her against him. There were no words that could make what had happened between them okay. She could never convince Easton that Lucas was the right choice. Or make him see that he could find someone better. They weren't there yet. Maybe they'd never get there. But she could give them both what they really needed—closure.

She took one more deep breath and then pulled back. This was good-bye. They both knew it. And they lingered over it for an extra minute. The end of an era.

Then, she gave him a small half-smile before walking back out the door and closing it firmly behind her. Where it belonged.

———

A CHILL RAN down her spine as she approached the landing of her former apartment building. Today had been illuminating, to say the least. But she wasn't looking forward to this final confrontation any more than she had looked forward to the others. She felt cracked open. Like an egg left out on a hot summer day. She didn't know if she'd end up over easy or rotten. Part of her didn't want to find out.

But she couldn't walk away from this with Lucas either. She'd given him no reason not to be mad. She'd wanted to ease him into the news. And then by the time they were finished screaming at each other, she'd realized she should have led with saying that she and Easton were over and she only wanted Lucas. Who could have known her honesty was going to be the real problem?

Not that he'd *asked* what she'd said. But she should have volunteered the information. Instead, she'd let her anger rise to the occasion. She couldn't do that now.

She sighed as she stepped outside into the oppressive heat and found him sitting on the stoop, staring out at the passing vehicles.

"Mind if I have a seat?" she asked, lightly nudging him with her toe.

He glanced up at her with raw anguish on his face. "Please do. Savannah, I—"

She stopped him again with a shake of her head before taking a seat on the stairs. She looked straight ahead, trying to decide where to begin. "Why do we keep doing this?"

He sighed heavily. "I don't know. Because we care about each other too much."

"Is it always going to be this way?"

He paused before responding, "No. I don't want to hurt you."

"I know," she said.

Because, of course, he didn't want to. But somehow, they kept hurting each other. It was a sick cycle that she didn't know how to break.

"I am sorry, Savannah," Lucas said. "I should have never yelled at you or run out of that apartment or done any of it. I've been trying so hard to be better for you...for us. And then I go and fuck it all up again."

"You know...you never asked me what I said to Easton when he said that he wanted us to get back together...that he still loved me."

Lucas swallowed. His Adam's apple bobbing. "I think...part of me didn't want to know. I couldn't bear to hear that you wanted to go back with him."

She finally turned her gaze to meet his. "Why would you think that I did?"

"I was second best to him for three years," he said with a sad shrug. "I wanted it to be different, but my brain kept telling me that I'd fuck it up. That you'd decide on the sensible choice. You'd go back to him now that he'd asked you to."

"The crazy thing is...that Easton has felt second best to you for nearly that long too."

Lucas frowned. "Yeah, well, the only thing I could think was that if I confronted him, then I could make it stop. That if he'd manned up and confronted me years ago, maybe I would have stopped."

"Would you have?" she asked curiously.

"You know…probably not."

She laughed softly. Because she knew he wouldn't have stopped. Not for a second. "I think Easton was right. I think he was second best to you all those years. No matter what I said." She looked up into his eyes. "My heart knew it was you."

"It was always you, Savi."

Tears welled in her eyes at the impossibility of this situation. Things weren't okay. She knew that they couldn't keep doing this to each other. She'd never survive the fighting or anger. But she loved him. She knew she did in that moment more than she ever had. Something she had never admitted to him or anyone else, let alone herself. But she knew it now. At the worst possible time.

"Don't cry," he whispered. He brushed the tears off of her cheeks. "Please, don't cry, Savi. We'll figure this out."

"I think all we've done is prove each other right. I knew you didn't want me to see Easton, but I saw him anyway. And you knew I wanted us to be calm about all this, and still, you acted rashly. Despite how amazing it'd been the last couple of weeks, we still ended up here." She swallowed back her tears. She didn't want to cry in this moment. She wanted answers. Answers that she didn't have. A choice she didn't want to have to make. "Where do we go from that, Lucas? Because I really don't know."

"Just because we've messed up doesn't mean that we give up. We would never have ever been together if we'd given up so easily. And I can't give up on you, Savi. I won't."

"Do you ever think that we just have too much baggage?" she asked him hollowly.

"No. I think we have history. And history can be good, and it can be bad. But it doesn't have to repeat itself." He placed his hand on hers. "Look at me."

She slid her gaze to his.

"If you think that I'm going to walk away because you talked to Easton, you're wrong. Do I like it? No. But I said I'm going to fight for you, Savannah, and I am. I said I wanted this to be different, and it will be."

"This feels the same," she told him honestly.

Lucas slowly rose to his feet. Then, he held his hand out to her and hoisted her up. "It's not the same. We're in an adjustment period. We've never done this before. Not together. I think we should give it more than two weeks before saying it all feels the same."

"But...you really thought I'd get back together with Easton? After everything?" she couldn't help but ask.

"Did you really think I'd go on the road and sleep with a bunch of groupies because I was bored?" he challenged.

"No," she said.

"Good, because I'd never do that. Every girl before you was just me trying to forget you. Now that I have you…I can't imagine ever looking at someone else."

She laughed, swiping at her eyes again. "God, why is this so stupid?"

"Because I'm crazy about you."

"I wish it didn't drive us both crazy."

He sighed and ran a hand back through his hair. "The way I see it, we have two choices going forward. One, now that everything is out in the open, we find a way to work this out to be together. Or two…we walk. I think that choice is yours."

"Lucas…"

"It's yours, Savi. You already know what I want."

"Tell me," she insisted.

"I could never walk away from you," he said, sliding a hand around her waist and tugging her a little closer. "I'll do whatever it takes to be the man you deserve. Look, I could have gone in there and punched Easton like I wanted, but I held back."

She snorted. "Oh, you poor thing. You didn't get to punch someone."

"Do you know how long I've wanted to punch him?"

"Please shut up," she said with a laugh and a shake of her head.

"Well, I've told you my choice."

"I'm not walking away, Lucas. I think we can work

on this, but I don't know how. I feel like getting it all out in the open is the first step. But it's so easy to fall back into old routines and fears."

"Then, maybe…we need to start over."

She furrowed her brow. "Didn't we do that?"

"Yes, and no. I was thinking more like…we should get away from the world and focus on us. What we really want and need. Rather than just pushing it aside with everything that's happening in the real world."

"Is this a con to get me to go on vacation with you?"

His fingers threaded up into her hair. The intensity in that stare almost unnerved her. "I want us to work. I want us to get that trust back. If that means I take you on vacation for a few days…then that seems okay with me."

"With your shiny, new bonus check?"

He caressed her cheek. "Better to put it to good use, spoiling my girl."

"What about work? I can't get days off on short notice."

"How about Labor Day weekend then?"

She didn't have any other objections. Really, she didn't have *any* objections. She desperately wanted this to work out with Lucas. But her resolve had been cracked and her fears exposed. She was terrified to keep trying and having her heart broken over and over. But if she didn't try, she'd regret it for the rest of her life.

"Where would we go?"

And he smiled, realizing that he had her. "I know just the place."

26

Hilton Head Island

Hilton Head had always felt like Savannah's summer escape. The place she went to get away from the world and reconnect. It was the site of many memorable family vacations. But she'd never actually been out here alone. Not until this weekend with Lucas.

She stepped out onto the back deck as Lucas brought their suitcases in. She breathed in the salty air with relief. The last two weeks had been…slow. They'd been taking things slow. What had happened with Easton had shown them both that they needed to be more conscious, more present. As much as she wanted to dive headfirst into all the physical again, she knew they'd kind of used it as an excuse. It was something they were already good at.

She blushed when she thought of it.

Really, really good at.

And while they'd known each other their whole lives, they had spent the last four years in different cities. Which left a lot of gaps in what they knew about each other. She wanted her best friend back as much as her boyfriend. And the gradual merging of the two felt like sweet relief.

The second she put her toes in the sand though, she knew Lucas had been right. No matter how much time they spent together in DC, they needed this retreat. A chance to get away, just the two of them.

"Putting your feet in the sand without me I see," Lucas said, stepping out onto the deck.

She whirled around with a smile. "Priorities."

He kicked his shoes off and walked down the few steps to stand at her side. "I love this place."

She reached for his hand and laced their fingers together. "Me too."

"Come on. Let's dip our toes in the water."

She laughed. "Nuh-uh. I know better."

He pulled her toward the waterline. "Come on. Just like old times."

"Lucas Atwood, you let me go right now."

"Just a quick dip. Just our toes."

She narrowed her eyes at him playfully. "I know all your tricks."

He laughed and dragged her in for a kiss. "Are you sure?"

"Definitely."

"What about this one?" he asked and then picked her up and threw her over his shoulder.

She screamed as he darted down toward the ocean. "Lucas, put me down!"

But she was laughing. Even as she beat on his back to get him to stop.

"It'll be fun," he said as he stepped his toes into the water for the first time.

And still, he didn't stop.

"Oh my God, what are you doing?" she shrieked.

Then, he tumbled forward, throwing both of them into the water. She went under, fully dressed, still in the jean shorts and white tank she'd worn to the airport. She came up, sputtering. Her clothes soaked through. Her hair a wet, salty mess. God only knew what her makeup looked like.

Then, Lucas launched himself at her, pulling her above the next wave that crested.

"You asshole," she said with a glimmer in her eye.

Then, she was laughing and laughing and laughing. She didn't remember the last time she had laughed this hard. Her stomach hurt as she doubled over to try to catch her breath.

"I cannot believe you just did that."

He winked. "Can't you though?"

"Fine. I can, but you are so going to pay for that later."

"I look forward to it."

He pulled her hard against him and crushed their

lips together. She opened herself to him, letting their tongues meet in the middle. And just then, another wave crashed over her head.

She coughed as salt water filled her mouth and gagged as it clogged her nose and stung her eyes. Then, it was Lucas's turn to laugh hysterically as he spat up the water.

"I guess we had that one coming," he said.

"*You* had that one coming."

She splashed him. And he dove for her. They both went under again. Her laughter was contagious. She felt so free out here with Lucas, acting like children. They had no one to impress. And though she was definitely going to get him back for throwing her in the ocean, she was kind of glad they'd started out this weekend on a silly note. Rather than a serious one.

"I'm going to need a shower," she said sometime later when they hauled themselves out of the water.

"You do that. Take your time, getting ready. I have a surprise for you."

She arched an eyebrow. "Oh?"

He winked and smacked her butt. "Go on. Get ready. When you're done, I'll show you."

"You know waiting is agony."

He snorted. "You'll live."

She kissed him one more time and then dashed upstairs. She peeled off her sopping wet clothes and then took a long, steaming shower. It took her forever to blow out her long hair, and then she went with soft, beachy makeup—a hint of mascara, blush, and a pink lipstick. She pulled on a teal sundress that hit just above her knees and came downstairs to find Lucas in khakis and a linen button-up, holding a box in his hand.

"Well, don't you look nice?" she said with a smile.

He grinned back at her. "You look gorgeous."

She glanced at the box in his hand. "Is that my surprise?"

"Yes, and no." He held out his hand. "I'll show you."

She was too curious not to take his hand, and she let him lead her back outside. The air was crisp with a slight breeze that softened the early September temperatures. She shivered a little, and Lucas wrapped an arm around her shoulders.

They left their shoes on the deck before continuing on into the sand. As they walked, she noticed candlelight in the distance. Her heart skipped a beat when she realized where they were walking toward... and what that candlelight signified.

"Our sand dune?" she asked a little breathlessly.

He grinned. "It's where it all started."

This was the place they had first been together after high school graduation. The place that belonged to them. So many memories were attached to it. And she could just see all the new memories they could make here.

They stopped in front of their sand dune. Lucas

must have come out here when she was showering and set up. There were a few dozen candles around a quilted blanket that she'd seen in the house before. A bottle of champagne was chilling in a bucket next to a small picnic basket.

"You didn't have to do this," she whispered, swallowing back the emotions threatening her.

"No, I did," he assured her.

He gestured for her to take a seat, and she sank down against the blanket. He followed her, pouring each of them a glass of champagne and then pulling out a makeshift charcuterie board with meat, assorted cheeses, and grapes. They nibbled on the fare before them for a few silent minutes before Lucas passed her the small box he'd been carrying with him.

She carefully set her champagne down before ripping open the wrapping paper. She laughed when she saw what it was. The same red frame that he had given her at graduation. With the ticket to *Seven Brides for Seven Brothers* from high school on one side and a picture of her and Lucas from that night with his arm over her shoulders while she held a giant bouquet that he'd given her.

She held it to her chest. "Thank you. I wanted to keep it the first time."

He swept a lock of hair behind her ear. "I know you did. I wanted things to be different then, but I see now that they couldn't be. Not yet. I'm glad you gave it back…so that I could give it to you now. I remember that night so well."

"You do?"

He nodded. "You love performing. You were bursting with energy. There was hope in that night. When I hugged you after this picture was taken, I thought about kissing you. Both of us were single for the first time in a while. And you looked up at me, so happy, so expectant. I thought, *Damn, I'm finally going to do it.*"

"But you didn't."

"Nope. Chickened out," he said with a laugh. "But it was the first time I thought maybe you'd let me."

Savannah stared down at the younger version of herself. "I would have let you," she told him. "Even though I thought it was a bad idea."

"Well, I didn't know that then." He pressed a kiss to her lips. "But I do now."

"I'm glad we did this. You were right. We needed this fresh start."

"I actually think I was wrong."

She laughed. "How so?"

"We didn't need a fresh start. We needed to be reminded of who we once had been before we screwed it all up. Because those are the people who are going to make it last. As the one who treasured you so much, I didn't risk a kiss because I couldn't lose you." He looked deep into her eyes. The flames from the candles igniting his irises. "But I want to change one thing, if that's all right with you?"

"And what is that?"

"Four years ago, we sat on this beach and decided to risk it all. Then, we left, went to separate cities and separate lives. Neither of us were bold enough then to ask for what we wanted. But I am now, Savannah," he told her bluntly. "I want you. And I want to make all those promises I should have made four years ago."

Savannah touched his hand. Her throat closed up at his declaration. She wanted to reach out and kiss him. How long had she wanted to hear those words? And now, they were finally here, in this moment. It almost felt too good to be true.

"I promise to cherish you above all others," he told her. He pressed a kiss onto her hand. "I promise to come to you first with my fears. I promise to listen to yours…to listen to you. I promise that I won't be perfect, but I'll try to be perfect for you."

She laughed, more of a hiccup through the happy tears that were coming to her eyes. "Lucas…"

"I promise to spend the rest of my days with you. If you'll have me?"

"Yes," she whispered.

"I promise to love you forever."

She choked on her tears, pushing forward to cup his jaw and press a kiss against his lips. "I promise to love you forever," she repeated.

He smiled. "I promise you forever."

She closed her eyes and smiled. Forever. It was quite a promise. But it was also somehow perfect. What they should have promised each other all those years ago. It was a blessing that they were here now… prepared to make these promises. Not an engagement, no ring…they weren't ready for that. But still… a promise to work together, to be together, and to love together. The best promise she could have asked for.

His hands went up into her hair as their kiss intensified. As the promises they'd made washed over them. They lay back against the blanket on the sand dune where it had all started and took their time reacquainting themselves with each other. Their clothes fell to the side. Lips and hands were greedy with want. She stroked him, begged him, wanted him. They came together seamlessly, him fitting inside her as if they had been made for this very moment. He was slow, painfully, achingly slow. Pulling back to wondrously watch her face as he began to move within her.

"Please," she pleaded, wanting more, so much more.

But he was content to hear her beg and still take his time. Drawing out her pleasure in a way she never could have imagined before tonight. As their promises drove this moment onward and onward. Her heart raced, and she felt her climax was so close. She could almost reach out and grab it.

Then, they were hitting that point together.

Coming undone and unraveling back into the sand. Becoming altogether something new from the force of their declarations.

And she knew then that some promises would be harder than others to maintain. Their problems wouldn't disappear overnight after all. But others would be so easy. So damn easy.

Like loving him forever.

She lay back in the sand with a sigh and stared into his beautiful eyes.

Oh yes, she could keep that promise with ease.

Epilogue

SIX MONTHS LATER

Savannah rushed forward into the waiting room. "Did you hear anything? Is my nephew here?"

Lucas ran into the room after her. "News?"

Savannah's mother, Marilyn, just calmly shook her head. "Nothing yet."

"You could have texted," Andrea said from the corner where she was hunched over a worn romance novel.

"We did. No one answered," Lucas said. He shucked off his peacoat, brushing errant snow off the shoulders.

"Cell service is shit," Clay said. He was positioned against the opposite wall of Andrea with a bored expression on his face. "We've been here all day. Gigi keeps getting pissed that I won't respond to her."

"Clay Alexander," Marilyn said with a huff. "Can you not with the language?"

Clay smiled like a Cheshire cat. "Sure, Mom."

"Oh Lord, we all know that smile," Savannah said, passing off her jacket to Lucas. "He's going to say every French word he knows in the next hour just to irritate you."

"I did give birth to him. You'd think I'd learn."

Her father, Jeff, stood with a laugh. "That does sound like our son." He pulled Savannah in for a hug. "Good to see you, sweetheart."

"You too."

He moved to shake hands with Lucas while Savannah settled into a seat between her mother and Andrea.

"So seriously, nothing from Brady or anything?"

"Unfortunately, no," Marilyn said.

"And he had to be born in a snowstorm," she said with a sigh.

"At least it's a weekend that I'm in town. I would have hated to miss this," Lucas said, crossing to shake hands with Clay.

"A miracle that he actually came on his due date," Andrea agreed.

"It's like he really *is* Brady's kid," Clay said sarcastically.

"Punctual?" Savannah teased.

Clay raised an eyebrow. "Goody-goody."

"Jealous?"

He laughed. "Every family needs a black sheep."

"Oh look, you've finally accepted your place."

"You two," Marilyn said with an eye roll. "Jeff, say something."

"Let them fight. It's more interesting than the silence," Jeff said.

Lucas snorted. "And it's good-natured. I've seen Clay fight dirty."

Savannah raised her eyebrows at him. "And you think Clay would win this fight?"

"Oh no. Now, you're in the doghouse," Clay said, nudging his shoulder.

Lucas just grinned. "We all know you're feisty. But Clay is a scoundrel."

"True story," Andrea said.

Clay shrugged. "I take no offense to this."

Her mother looked like she was about to say something again when the door finally opened. Everyone launched to their feet as Brady appeared in the open doorway. He looked sleep-deprived yet elated. His heart was on his sleeve, and a smile lit up his face.

"We have a baby boy!" Brady said. "Brady Jefferson Maxwell IV. We're calling him Jefferson."

Everyone jumped to their feet at once. A string of congratulations went around the room. Hugs were given. Her mother began to cry in earnest.

"Our first grandchild," she kept saying over and over again to her husband.

He put his arm around her and tugged her close.

"When can we meet him?" Savannah asked.

"Now," Brady said with a smile. "We've had some time together. They just moved Liz into a room with him. They said it's time everyone could come meet him."

Together, they walked down the hallway through the labor and delivery department of Sibley Memorial Hospital in downtown DC. Lucas reached out and took her hand in his as they entered the private suite that had been set up for Liz. There was joy on his face too. Joy for a new baby in their life. Joy that they'd made it to this moment. Joy for the ring on her finger that said he was finally joining her family.

He twirled the ring in a circle absentmindedly. He'd taken to doing that. And she liked it.

The day he'd proposed, he'd flown her into Charlotte while he was there for a game. Then, they drove back home to Chapel Hill. While her family came together where they'd grown up, Lucas took her on the back deck. They sat on the porch swing, huddled together against the cold. Then, he got down on one knee and asked her to be his wife.

"Yes," was the only word she'd had for him.

And it felt like another promise.

The real promise they'd been speaking about all those months before. So, six weeks, six months, six years…it didn't matter how long it had taken to get to this moment. All that mattered was that they were there, and they'd kept their promises.

She followed him into the room and found a

groggy-looking Liz holding the tiniest little bundle against her chest. Her cheeks were flushed, her hair was askew, she was still wearing hospital clothing— and she was the most beautiful Savannah had ever seen her. She just glowed as she held her son.

Marilyn began to cry as she leaned over Liz to look at Jefferson. "Oh my goodness, the most precious gift in the world."

"Do you want to hold him?" Liz asked.

Marilyn nodded. "Yes, very much so."

Liz deftly passed Jefferson into Marilyn's arms, and then they all just stared at the little baby.

Liz laughed, breaking the spell. "I think I need a shower."

Brady chuckled. "That seems fair."

Savannah sat around with her family as Liz went to shower. Jefferson was passed from person to person. A little bundle of hot potato. And when he landed in her arms, she held him as gently as possible. Not that he seemed to mind a bit. He barely even moved, as tightly swaddled as he was. He just slept on, oblivious to the big world around him. Just new and fresh and ready for anything.

She glanced up when Liz finally reappeared in clean clothes with her wet hair piled high on her head. Then, she stood and passed Jefferson off to his mother.

A stillness came over the room. A sense of calm

like Savannah had never experienced before. A baby changed something…everything.

It made Savannah look at it all differently. Not that she was ready to have children by any means. She wanted to become a badass journalist before then. But still…he was a miracle. And beyond that, he made her look around her, at her own beautiful family, and she realized how damn lucky she was.

She had spent so long trying to escape being a Maxwell. Run away from the thing that made her different from everyone else. That made her special or important for no other reason than the family she had been born into.

But this was the life she had been given. It was a damn good one. And she didn't want to run away from it anymore. She was lucky to be a Maxwell. Whatever privileges that afforded was not the summation of her name. It was just the most public part of it all.

This, this right here, was what being a Maxwell meant. It meant family.

Lucas pulled her tight into his side as she gazed around at her family. At her mother and father, Clay and Andrea, Brady and Liz and baby Jefferson…and Lucas, the person she planned to spend the rest of her life with.

And she knew right where she belonged.

The End

Love Savannah & Lucas?
Get ready for a new second chance stand alone romance with Lark and Sam in…

THE
LYING SEASON

Walking away from Sam Rutherford was the hardest thing I've ever done. It's been five years since that day, and I've given up on looking for love. My focus is on my career.

Then Sam walks into my office as the new legal counsel. Which means I have to see him every single day. We vow to remain professional, but it's a small office. The sly glances and his blistering charm are unavoidable.

It all feels so familiar. Too comfortable. After what happened the first time…I should know better.

If I'm not careful, he'll break my heart all over again. And I don't know if I can survive Sam a second time.

Coming February 4th!

Acknowledgments

Thank you to everyone who encouraged me to write this story. And to everyone who read it month by month in my newsletter. It was a learning experience for us all. I can't thank you enough for loving Savannah's story as much as I do. And I hope you stick around to try *The Lying Season* coming February 4th!

About the Author

K.A. Linde is the *USA Today* bestselling author of the Wrights, Cruel series, and more than thirty other novels. She loves reading fantasy novels, binge-watching Supernatural, traveling to far off destination, baking insane desserts, and dancing in her spare time.

She currently lives in Lubbock, Texas, with her husband and two super-adorable puppies.

For exclusive content and free books every month.
www.kalinde.com/subscribe

CPSIA information can be obtained
at www.ICGtesting.com
Printed in the USA
LVHW091055201119
PP15395300001B/4/P